The Spirit of Giving

Despite pain and loss a family brings
joy to their community

VERA SMITH

Springs
CHRISTIAN
LITERATURE

ISBN 0 9549225 1 4

Published by
Springs Christian Literature
63 a Kilvergan Road,
Lurgan, BT66 6LJ
Northern Ireland
United Kingdom

List of Contents

Acknowledgements

I am grateful to Patricia Carson for writing the Preface: Dr. Brian Craig for his contribution: Jennifer Hampton, for her art: Vivienne Kerr, Patricia McCracken and Wendy Mitchell (leaders in Girl Guides and Brownies), and Diane McClelland (teacher), for stimulating their young people to compete in the drawing and colouring competitions. Congratulations to the talented young people whose art enhances this publication!

Thanks to those who posed for photographs with patience and tolerance: to the curator, Mr. Robert Heslop, and staff of Armagh Museum: to Inspector Urban Magee of the N. I. Railways and The Railway Preservation Society for their helpfulness - the guard uniform on Page 51 is Canadian, and was worn in 1800's.

Thanks to Jim and Gwen Kane, Florence Gamble and Laura Davidson for providing the setting at Blacker's Mill and for valuable information on the linen industry. To Mr. Gordon Lyttle for permission to use the drawing of Richhill Castle: to William Austin, Richard Gilpin and Laura Reilly for their photographic expertise. Thanks to William Burnett, Jonathan Conkey, Daphne Morrow and Eleanor Watkins for proofreading the manuscript.

I also want to express my sincere gratitude to George Russell, Denis Flanagan, Joe Costley and his staff, Mark Proctor, and others for their help and encouragement.

Foreword

If you picked up this book because you are already familiar with Vera Smith's writings then you know how her work has been greatly used to help so many people. It has been a delight to read this first publication in a completely different genre, that of cultural literature. We all have memories of books, which we enjoyed time and time again. I have no doubt this book will become a favourite.

Vera takes us on a journey into a world that is very dear to her - her roots. We have a delightful story, rich with themes, which make it a page turner, one which will be reached for at bedtime again and again. These themes, among which are the past, pets, friendships and Christmas, are woven into a wholesome, historically accurate story in which we become aware of Vera's love of local history and her firm faith. Her ability and desire to communicate this faith to all ages is clear.

It has been a privilege and indeed an education to be on this journey with Vera as she has brought this book into reality. Enjoy it and pass it on to your friends - they will find all kinds of riches in its pages.

Patricia Carson
Housewife, mother and schoolteacher.

Preface

When Mary Adele Clarke was twelve years of age, she gave me my favourite Christmas present - a good story!

Mary was an avid reader and when missing, she was usually in a quiet corner lost in a good book. When she had exhausted her children's books, she would devour adult literature. Her parents were teachers so there was opportunity to develop her interest with lots of good reading material in the house.

Mary's story was set at the end of the last world war, when a young mother and her three children faced their first Christmas without a father. It was a short story – just two A4 pages, neatly typed on both sides, but it painted a picture of the pain and hardship of families left to face the aftermath of war. It also opened a doorway to the future. Despite pain and loss, the Pringle family proved there is strength to cope no matter how difficult the circumstances.

Mary has allowed me to take my readers back to the early twentieth century, when the First World War robbed us of many precious fathers and sons. I have given it a local setting in one of Ireland's most beautiful counties, known as the Garden of Ulster. Trace our history, identify with our suffering, admire our progress, and get to know our people – we have a rich heritage!

I have appreciated all the comments from those who have waited to read this story. By popular request, I have included a number of poems, which I trust will satisfy the poetry enthusiasts.

The book is suitable for age groups 9 to 90, so put your feet up, sit back and relax as you read 'The Spirit of Giving'.

Vera Smith

Annie at the Window

A White World

It was Christmas Eve. In the Pringle home, the tinsel shimmered on the tree and a fresh aroma of falling pine needles filled the air. Annie Pringle peeked out of the steamy living room window. The snowflakes outside drifted slowly downwards forming a vast, white sheet on the damp ground below and the voices of the winter carollers rang out loud and clear. She pricked up her ears and heard the crisp footsteps of the mill workers through the snow – they looked forward to a cup of hot soup and a mug of cocoa or tea when they arrived home.

Annie turned round and watched her little sister and toddler brother excitedly hanging their stockings above the mantelpiece, for their long wait was over and tomorrow their dreams would come true! They would waken with excitement to discover a stocking full of sweets, an orange, an apple and small surprise parcels.

It had been an eventful Christmas Eve! Without disturbing Heidi and Benny, Annie slipped past them and sat down in Grandma's old rocking chair. So much had happened that it seemed more like a week than a day! There had been a build up of excitement all week as Heidi and Benny checked off the days to Christmas. Each morning they were wakening earlier - last night, Benny dreamt it was Christmas Day! At five o'clock, he rushed into Annie and Heidi, wakening them out of a deep sleep.

"C'rimas 'ide! C'rimas Annie!"

"P'esents! Come 'ide! Get 'ockin! Come 'ickly, 'ide!"

Poor Benny was so disappointed when he discovered he had to wait another day. Annie and Heidi had to bring him to the living room and show him that nothing had changed. Annie hugged Benny. "It's so difficult to wait, Benny, but it's not long now. Mama will be here soon and we will all have a special breakfast with bacon and eggs."

"ippy! 'ippy! Benny, 'ove b'eckfast."

Benny's excitement wakened Mama. Soon she and Annie were frying bacon and eggs for the family Christmas Eve treat: breakfast was always a family time in the Pringle home, but Christmas Eve was special and Mama would ensure it would not change this year.

"Let's give thanks for the food," said Mama Pringle when everyone had taken their seats around the table.

Replacing his fork beside the plate, Benny made a request –

"'ing Mama!"

"What do you want to sing?"

"Benny know 'esus 'oves me!"

"That's not suitable! Sing, 'All Good Gifts'," said Heidi. "We will sing 'Jesus Loves Me' later, Benny," but we want to thank the Lord for the food just now!" Annie started to sing and the others joined in...

"All good gifts around us are sent from Heaven above,
So thank the Lord; Oh, thank the Lord, for all His love."

The clock was striking eight o'clock as breakfast started. Mrs. Pringle looked at the clock and knew she would have to relax with her family over breakfast, while at the same time, it was important there was plenty of time to finish preparing for a big celebration on Christmas Day.

"Benny thought it was Christmas Day, Mama," said Heidi. There was laughter Benny told them his dream about Santa getting "'uck" coming down the chimney!

During school holidays, Annie always helped with the chores. She enjoyed working in the small kitchen with Mama, because not only did it ease the work load for Mama, but it gave them time to talk together.

Annie cleared the table and washed the breakfast dishes. A lengthy conversation followed.

"Perhaps I will be able to work in the mill next year Mama! I will be twelve in April, so Mr. Pepper might allow me work during the school holidays. I could earn some money to help you buy food and clothes for us all, while at the same time, learn more about weaving and the linen industry."

Papa often sat down on winter's evenings and talked to Annie about his work in the mill. He explained that the flax is a plant grown for its fibre and seed. Papa had told her that the fibre, grown around Millvale produced the linen fabric and a variety of other products including rope, high quality paper and thread – the seeds contained oil, called linseed oil, used in making paint and varnish."

Annie found it easy to express her thoughts and often was teased for 'thinking out loud!', but she did not mind.

"I suppose that is how Linseed got its name! Someone added the word 'seed' to the first three letters of linen and discovered linseed oil! It seems so simple, but it was a very clever person who discovered that the seed from the flax could be used to make paint and varnish."

Mrs. Pringle was deep in thought! Annie had brought to her mind vivid pictures of dear Jack before her. She was touched that Annie wanted to work at the mill to earn money to help her and felt a lump in her throat but managed to compose herself and respond to Annie's comments.

"Annie dear, you must not worry about me for you are young and need to learn as much as you can at school. You must enjoy your childhood for soon you will be facing adolescence. Papa would want you to benefit from your education. You have an excellent teacher in Miss Diane. I wish I had been more attentive at school for I would be able to help you with your homework: instead, you are helping me to understand and appreciate our village life. I remember Miss Hamley telling us about the farmers growing flax to produce the linen, but I never knew about the rope, thread, high quality paper and linseed oil."

Annie was surprised at her Mama's confession. She thought her Mama knew everything that Papa knew, but because she had so much work to do in the house she did not have the time to spend in talking about such subjects as flax and linen. Her Mama knew all about cooking and sewing and she always knew what medicines to give for tummy upsets and headaches. Annie did not want her Mama to feel hurt by what she was telling her so quickly continued...

"Miss Diane told us that flax also has some medical uses!"

Mrs. Pringle sensed Annie's hesitation and responded by asking her to tell her more.

"The Linen industry was woven into our family life. When your Papa left school, he went to work in the mill. There were no other jobs in Millvale, apart from becoming a 'farm hand' - only the 'white collar men' travelled to the towns and cities to work. Your Papa came from a farming background, but seemed to adapt quickly to working in the mill where he quickly learned the trade and passed his knowledge on to others. When the machines broke down, there was someone on our doorstep, so that he was always on call. Now that Papa is no longer with us, I want to know more about it."

Mrs. Pringle looked at the clock. She could not believe that an hour had passed!

Even though it was Christmas Eve, she must wash Benny's socks, and trousers and Heidi's dress for church on Christmas morning.

Mama brought out the tub and the washboard.

"Where is the ˙yellow soap, Annie?"

Annie had used the soap and forgotten to put it back in the usual place. She apologized to Mama and quickly brought both the soap and the ˙blue bag to Mama.

˙ YELLOW SOAP:

At the turn of the 19th century, a large bar of yellow soap was used for washing clothes. Each garment was placed over the washboard, and the soap rubbed over it: then the dirt was removed, by vigorously rubbing the garment up and down over the ridges on the washboard. It was then rinsed, in another big tub, and hung on the line to dry.

˙ BLUE BAG:

• The blue bag was a small blue detergent type bar in a muslin bag - all the white clothes needed a quick dip of the blue bag to make sure they were crisp and white.

• Another use for the blue bag was to whiten the wash to paint the cottage. It was dipped in the bucket of whitewash to ensure a brilliant white finish to paint the outside of the cottages.

Facts about the Flax Industry

Flax Flowers

- The climate in Ireland is most suitable for growing flax because it grows best in cool, moist climates with rainy summers.
- The variety grown for fibre has a slender stem and seed flax is bushier than fibre flax and bears more seeds.
- Harvesting: It is in the spring after the danger of frost is past the seed is sown, then after three to four months, it is harvested. The whole family helps to pull the stalks out of the ground. If harvested too early, the fibre will be silky and not suitable for manufacturing.

- Retting: After harvesting the flax, the stems are soaked in water. Flax can be retted by soaking in a tank, a river, or laying it out on the grass in thin layers to allow dew, rain and the warmth of the sun to 'ret' the flax stems. The farmers place large stones on top of the flax to keep it under the water – the flax stalks have to be kept under the water for five nights. After five days, the fibre is spread out to dry for a few days: only when it is dry is it ready for breaking and *scutching."

Flax Thread

- Scutching was a process whereby the woody part of the flax was separated from the fibre, by pounding. Wealthy flax growers had scutch mills where local farmers brought their flax to the mill for scutching.
- Some of our senior citizens remember their grandmother telling them how they had to rise two hours earlier and work for their fathers in the scutch mill before going to school!

(Information on Flax industry courtesy of Florence Gamble)

Retting the Flax

Teddybear Toby

In the mid morning when Annie was busily helping Mama in the kitchen, she heard sad singing coming from the neighbour's garden. What could possibly be wrong in the Begley family?

Annie went to the back door to see what was going on. She saw Joey, Bessie and Tom Begley making their way through the deep snow singing 'The Lord's my Shepherd'. Joey was carrying a small box, Bessie and Tom were singing softly as they walked slowly behind him. Annie climbed over the lower part of the fence. She soon realized what had happened. Before the Christmas holidays, Bessie had told her at the close of class, on the last day at school, that Toby had not been well during the week, but she thought it was just a winter cold. Nothing was said as Annie took her place beside her best friend, Bessie. There were tears in Bessie's eyes as she whispered,

"Toby died last night! Annie".

Toby was their cuddly little puppy - known to everyone in Millvale as 'Teddybear Toby'!

Teddybear Toby

Annie solemnly joined the procession and respectfully shared the Begley sorrow. Bessie was comforted by Annie, as she reminded her that Toby would always be remembered.

"In the spring when the bluebells and primroses come up at the bottom of your garden, we will have such happy memories of all the fun we had with Toby. Now he has a beautiful resting place, Bessie!"

Bessie and Annie stopped and looked back to the bottom of the garden. Bessie was still tearful as they stood together for a short while without speaking. It had stopped snowing and the view at the back was beautiful as the sun lit up the hill beyond the village, where old man Gregg lived. Suddenly it struck Annie that old man Gregg had a little dog the same as Toby – they were the same litter of pups, possibly identical twins, but Bertie Donaghy, the breeder, was not sure, as he was away to market when they were born. Annie had an idea...

"Bessie when the spring comes, we will climb up to old man Gregg's cottage on the hill and see Toby's brother."

Bessie thought it might help her later, but now she was not thinking about anything other than her 'Teddybear' Toby.

Old Man Gregg's House on the Hill

"You must come into my house so that we can talk together, Bessie," said Annie as they waded their way back through the snow. The tears were rolling down Bessie's cheeks as she asked Joey and Tom to tell her Mama and Papa she was with her friend Annie next door. She knew they would understand her sorrow and loss and that Annie would be able to comfort her. The two girls walked slowly into the kitchen to Mama Pringle who took the weeping girl in her arms and tried to console her. No words were spoken, but Bessie dried her tears as she felt the strength of dear Mama Pringle's arms encircle her.

"He was such a cuddly little puppy!" said Bessie as Mama Pringle gave her a hot cup of cocoa and freshly baked cookie.

"I will miss my 'Teddybrear Toby', but as long as I have my good friend Annie, things will be fine!"

The hint of a smile broke out on Bessie's face as the two girls left the kitchen to have a 'heart-to-heart' chat in Annie's bedroom: they crept on tiptoe past the door where Heidi and Benny were playing with their toys. The door was open and they knew that if Heidi and Benny spotted them, they would want to join them. As they entered the bedroom, Annie spotted Benny's shoes. He had carried them in, early in the morning, leaving them in the middle of the floor. Suddenly, Annie bit her lip and thought of the day 'Teddybear Toby' had chewed on Benny's sandals and swallowed the buckle. Uncle Ben had bought the sandals for Benny's second birthday, but they were short lived! Secretly she wondered if Toby had died as a result of swallowing the buckle, but did not dare reveal her secret fear to Bessie.

When the two girls were comfortably seated, Annie asked Bessie to tell her what happened to Toby. She was greatly relieved when she discovered that swallowing the buckle had nothing to do with Toby's death. Bessie explained that he had eaten poison on farmer Brown's farm on the other side of the river. Farmer Brown had left poison for rats that had raided his barn and destroyed his grain. When the boys took Toby for a walk along the far river bank, over the stile to farmer Brown's house, they let him off the lead. The wee puppy was so delighted to be free, that he bounded forward and was gone like a flash. He dashed past farmer Brown and his son in the yard and disappeared into the granary. It was not until Toby became ill that they realized what had happened. Bessie and Annie sobbed together. It was Annie who spoke first! She knew she would have to help Bessie — she must have a happy Christmas, and it was up to Annie to help her through her grief. Annie had gone through the loss of her dear father, so knew that if she could cope with the death of a precious father, Bessie could cope with the loss of Toby.

Annie began to tell Bessie, about a story she read during the summer holidays. It was about a girl called Frances Ridley Havergal. She was a clever child. At four years of age she could read any book correctly. As the youngest child in a family of six, she had found herself alone much of the time, so she developed a special bond with her little puppy. She loved Flora dearly, just the way Bessie loved Toby. It was while her family lived for a short time in a big mansion, called Henwick House, that little Flo, as she was affectionately known, died. Frances was heartbroken. She often walked through the gardens with Flo, so when she died she buried her under a tree in the back lawn. At that time, she wrote:

"Here lies little Flora. Died, April 16, 1844.
Aged 7. Reverence her remains."

Flo was buried under a tree in the back lawn.

"Frances cherished that little piece of paper, as it seemed to help her cope with the loss of her puppy. You should write something like that in memory of Toby! Often when we do something physical, it helps us work through our grief. Another good way to cope with losing someone or something special is to help somebody, or, do something positive - as Papa used to say, 'improve your knowledge'. Frances decided to move forward and dedicated herself to learning French and German and writing poetry and prose, while still a child. Although she never had a governess, she progressed rapidly and became fluent in both languages."

"Oh Annie, you are so wise and helpful. I will do that. Thank you so much! You always give me the right advice."

The girls knew the amount of work their Mamas had to get through, so they hurried back to help with the Christmas Day preparations.

Papa Pringle and Millvale

Still gently rocking on Grandma's old chair, Annie watched Heidi put Suzy into the pram. What joy she had when she was the same age as Heidi and came down one Christmas morning to discover Santa had brought her a pram for her treasured Suzy. The pram was made of wood. It was silver grey with a pretty design painted in pink, green and yellow and the hood was pale blue. The tiny wheels and the handle were brown, also made of wood.

She remembered clearly the day she took the pram outside for the first time. The snow had melted but the ground was still wet. Suzy was 'as snug as a bug in a rug', tucked in her warm blanket. Mama peeped in and said she looked pretty in her new pram. Because Papa had cleared the snow from the area outside the back door, the winter sun had dried that area, but as soon as she ventured a few yards from the house, the tiny wooden wheels stuck in the deep snow. She struggled for a long time trying to pull the pram out of the snow, but reluctantly gave up and, lifting Suzy out of her pram, she picked up the pillow and blanket to go for help. Just as she wistfully looked back at the pram, Papa arrived, lifted the pram and carried it into the house. Mama helped her to clean it while Papa planned to make a new set of wheels that would be much larger for taking Suzy outside in her new pram.

Annie enjoyed watching her father make the big round wooden wheels. He knew exactly what to do and cut four pieces of wood, used his saw to cut off the corners and then skillfully he filed the wood - carefully following the pencil lines he had drawn on the wood to form a circle.

"Papa, I think Santa must have made my pram himself," Annie had commented, as Papa filed the wood to shape the round wheels.

"You are right, Annie," Papa said with a smile on his face! "I have never seen another pram like it!"

As Annie rocked back and forth, she thought of the hours Mama had spent that winter knitting a blanket and making a pillow for the pram. Neighbours and relations gathered the feathers from the chickens to stuff the pillow! She had also made clothes for Suzy, as well as knitting jumpers for the family. What a happy family they had been! Annie had given Suzy to Heidi on her last birthday. Although she still enjoyed playing with Suzy, she was happy that Heidi was getting so much pleasure from her precious doll. Annie watched Heidi take Suzy over to Mrs. Black's Sweet Shop in the corner of the room to buy sweets.

"Two ounces of Dolly Mixtures please Mrs. Black," said Heidi.

Because Mama had bought real sweets for a treat on Christmas Eve, the children were able to enjoy their purchase at the shop. Heidi settled down on the mat beside Benny to share her sweets. She gave Benny a few in his hand for she knew if she gave him too many they would all go into his mouth at the same time. Benny was learning fast from his big sister but he was still only a baby to his caring sisters. Heidi then offered some to Suzy and asked her if she liked Mama's special Christmas Eve treat. Of course, Suzy was delighted! Annie's thoughts went back to the year Santa brought her the sweet shop. It too was made of wood, with red and gold lettering over the windows and door – *'Mrs. Black's Sweet Shop'*.

Annie and Mama had made fake sweets, so it was fun to pretend to buy and eat sweeties. One jar was for real sweets – it contained 'Dolly Mixtures' and was only filled for special occasions like Christmas, Easter and birthdays. The money looked real: the coins were made of cardboard and the notes were paper. *The five pound notes looked just like the note Papa received in his Christmas pay packet! The whole family sometimes joined in and had lots of fun playing shop. Annie's arithmetic improved! She became skilled in counting the money and giving Heidi the change. Heidi improved so much that she went from near the bottom of the class to number two in arithmetic. Jane Denby, the 'brain box' knew she would have to work hard to keep top of the class! The coins were so like the real money that Heidi was convinced they were real - they were much larger than real money, so that Benny would not put them in his mouth. Heidi was in another world! She could spend hours with her 'pretend shop'.

The shop reminded Annie of Mrs. Annie Byrnes' shop in Millvale. As she watched Heidi, she remembered Papa playing shop with her – one day she asked him if Santa had ever been to the grocery shop in the village!

"Annie, you amaze me!" She could almost hear him say it and could visualize the expression on his face as he burst into laughter, and continued... "You seem to work out solutions to all your questions!"

Papa was always truthful with Annie and knew she was beginning to ask more questions about the traditions of her ancestors and about the true values in life.

He was cautious in replying...

"Yes, Annie, he must have liked Millvale, therefore he thought you would like a shop you could associate with home. Indeed, it is very like Mrs. Annie Byrnes' shop down the street: it has the same windows and even the writing on the board above the windows is the same. He did design it on Mrs. Byrne's shop!"

Papa loved the village of Millvale. Although the job was mundane and he often wished for a change, he had grown to love life in the closely knit community, and chose his wife from the Millvale girls - it was through working with Adam Richardson in the mill he met his daughter Mary and that was the happiest day of his life. It was 'love at first sight', and soon he had 'his feet under the table'! The Richardson family came to the area at the start of the linen boom in Ireland so Adam had a profound knowledge of the trade. Sadly, he lost his business through unfortunate family circumstances, and had to work for Mr. Pepper, but he had a wealth of knowledge on the growth of flax and the development of Irish linen. Grandpa Richardson could trace his family back to the start of the weaving industry in the country: this meant that Annie inherited her interest from both her Grandpa and her Papa – they had passed on a lot of historical knowledge, so everywhere she went she could picture her Mama's family background in the village.

The picturesque village of Millvale was nestled in a fertile valley with a meandering river that was the life- blood to the heart of Ulster. Surrounded on the east and west by undulating hills, that provided luscious grass for cattle and sheep, the village had its own unique character, though similar to many of the mill villages throughout Ireland. The fields were small with dividing hedges: here and there, an occasional tree provided shelter for the animals. Millvale had the advantage of being near a large town** that was fast becoming industrialized.

Jack and Mary Pringle's parents and grandparents often talked about the changes they had lived through and of 'the good old days' when they survived severe winters without a complaint and neighbours helped each other when 'times were tough'. Mary's father and grandfather remembered the eighteen boats navigating the river in 1836. Some of them docked beside the mill giving spectators entertainment as they unloaded coal, flour and oatmeal and loaded the linen back into the boats to be taken to England and across the world. Adam Richardson and John Abraham Adams were close friends. John was the village blacksmith, who not only knew his trade, he was a mine of information on the history of Millvale: he had to be ready every day for the horse-drawn boats to dock at Millvale for most of them needed his services after the long haul along the Tow path. He talked to the boatmen and exchanged news, then passed it on to the farmers when they brought their horses to the blacksmith's shop, to friends at social gatherings, and around the fireside in winter. John Adams thought the boatmen may have added to their tales of life on the river boats, but they sounded authentic - apart from their 'fishy' tales of the weight of the big trout caught during their lunch break!

Life in Millvale was not dull. The boatmen always waved to the villagers on their way through the port and when they left with their boats laden with linen. Some occasionally threw sweets or apples to the children, shouting, 'Finders! Keepers'!

Mr. Pepper, the mill owner had two special events each year. There was the Annual Sports day at the end of June and the Christmas party on the last day of the school year. Both events were highlights in the life of the village and were part of the school calendar. They were social occasions, as parents and friends met to enjoy a chat and relax in a friendly community atmosphere: for the children there was competition and fun, so that the occasion was a treat for everyone. Each child received a party bag - it contained two apples and a small toy: everyone received a bag with two sandwiches, a bun and a bar of chocolate.

The railway line was close to the village, but there was no station. Those who worked in the nearby town and in the big city, left very early in the morning by pony and trap: some were known to beg a boat ride on the early morning*** river boat, laden with imports to catch the first train heading north.

Footnotes

* £5, at the beginning of the 1900's would be equivalent to approximately £200 today!

Each bank had its own note similar in size and lay out, but in the middle of the 20th century, the Bank of England produced a large white five-pound note.

(Information courtesy of the former curator of Armagh Museum, Robert Heslop)

** In 1831 the town was not more than a small village, but the residents saw the potential of the waterway and by 1837 the town became a port with 745 residents. In 1838 history records, there were imports and exports by the river. Iron, coal, slates, flour and oatmeal amounted to 1,700 tons of imports. Wheat, oats and barley totalled 5,000 tons of exports. The development of a canal system boosted the whole economy of the area, besides providing work for villages along the river. *(Information from the writings of the late Henry Wolsey).*

*** The river flowed into Britain's largest inland waterway: then flowed out at the northern shore and coursed through farmlands, eventually flowing into the Atlantic Ocean at Coleraine.

The mill at Carrickblacker, had specialists in Damask hand weaving

Damask weaver at work in Blacker's mill in the mid fifties
(Photographs curtsey of Mr. and Mrs. J. Kane)

A Busy Time for Mama

As Annie recalled her conversation with Papa, she wished she could ask him about his family and life with Grandma and Grandpa Pringle, but she would have to wait until the next time she visited Uncle Ben on the farm. Benny, who had lost concentration, was upsetting Heidi by interrupting her thoughts. He wanted her to play with him, but Heidi was still having fun with Mrs. Black's Sweet Shop. Annie knew she would have to watch him because she did not want Mama to have to leave her work in the kitchen if he cried. He tried to build a wall with his wooden blocks, but was upset when the bricks tumbled down. Benny's frustration gave way to a loud scream, so Annie joined the toddler on the mat to sample the sweeties from Mrs. Black's Sweet Shop, and help Benny build a house with a chimney.

"Will Santa be able to get down the chimney?" Annie asked Benny.

"'Ook, 'eidi'! 'ook! 'eidi - Santa come down chim'e!" shouted Benny excitedly.

Heidi paid no attention to Benny's excitement for she was counting her pennies to pay for the sweets at the shop. She pretended Mrs. Black was in the shop and talked to her about the Christmas preparations.

"Mama made the steamed pudding earlier this afternoon - it smelled so good! I felt my tummy was empty but I knew Mama would not let me taste it so I had to come to buy more sweets!"

Mama was toiling in the kitchen in preparation for the next day. Annie knew she was making a lot of sacrifices to give them a happy time. She was right!

Mrs. Pringle wiped a stray tear from her eye as she mixed pastry. The air around was filled with the delicious smells of mince pies, turkey and cakes. The stove filled the kitchen with warmth as a pudding baked inside. Mrs. Pringle gazed down at the pint-sized turkey she had scraped and saved to afford. She sighed and turned back to her work. If only her brave husband had been there, rushing home from his dull, hard work to a happy home. He would be cheery, full of the festivities that Christmas brings. He was always teasing and jolly. How much he had given up for the family!

Mary was the only one who knew how bored he was at times – she had seen it in his discouraged and dim eyes, though he would have preferred to die rather than lay his burdens on his family. He was due for promotion in the mill and looked forward to a more responsible job with a better salary.

Now he was dead, one of the many whom the war had robbed of life!

How could she let her Jack become part of that cold, heartless war? Her loving honest Jack! Just then she was forced to push him out of her mind as a scream went up from the living room.

Mrs. Pringle rushed in, only to find Benny in a bad mood.

"WAH!" he wailed, prodding a chubby finger accusingly at Heidi. "She dwapt tweddy in the fwire!" "Me want tweddy!"

Mrs. Pringle scooped him up in her arms and comforted him.

"Hush, my darling!" She had brought a bun from the kitchen, so she gave it to Benny. It worked! Benny soon stopped crying and ate his bun.

He then settled down and was asleep in seconds in his mother's lap. Later on, a rather shamefaced Heidi came before her mother.

Annie saved the situation...

"Mama, please don't be cross with Heidi. She didn't mean it," Annie pleaded.

Annie had watched what had happened and knew that Heidi had left her own play to join her in keeping Benny occupied. As she threw the teddy in the air, he landed in the fire!

Mrs. Pringle was upset for she knew how much Benny loved his teddy, but it was Christmas Eve and her heart was tender towards her fatherless children. Annie's pleading eyes won the day! She smiled!

"Heidi, these things happen. Now hurry to bed, child. Tomorrow is a very important day."

Mrs. Pringle asked Annie to light a candle on the mantelpiece and give it to Heidi, who gladly disappeared down the hall! Meanwhile, Annie cleared away the toys and tidied the room for Christmas morning. Then she hung up her stocking before returning to the kitchen to see if she could help.

When Mama had the children safely tucked in bed, she returned to make the stuffing for the turkey. Annie watched the movement of her mother's hands. They were slightly red as she had been washing, cooking and cleaning all day. Just as she was about to ask for a job, she hesitated...

"Mama..." she began, "you shouldn't have pawned your wedding ring for Christmas dinner."

Mrs. Pringle swung round –

"Annie, what is the meaning of this? Have you been spying on me?"

"No Mama, but I saw it was missing from your finger... er! em! You always wear it, so I guessed you..."

"Annie you mustn't say a thing about this to anyone... I couldn't bear to let my family go without a treat at Christmas. There isn't a lot, but I've done my best."

"Papa and I loved our three children. You were God's special gift to us. On our wedding day your Papa gave me the ring as we both made a promise - 'until death do us part'. It was a precious moment! When I thought of the joy and happiness you all brought into our home, I knew I would have to do all I could to ensure that this first Christmas without Papa, would be a happy one. I did not have anything valuable only my gold wedding ring. It hurt, Annie, but I knew Papa would have done the same had he been left with our wedding ring. I did it for both of us!"

"Mama, I think I understand! You prove your love every day by your care of us, and what you have done, I will never forget! I promise I will keep our secret - nobody will ever know!"

Annie's offer of help was refused for Mama was about to clear the table to get it ready for the Christmas morning breakfast. She looked admiringly at her oldest daughter and felt she had grown years older since Papa died, nearly eight months ago. She lit a candle and gave it to Annie with a gentle smile – that smile conveyed to Annie the love and devotion of a faithful and caring mother.

"Now take this candle child, and be off to bed. It's getting late."

Annie gave her a hug and hurried away, clutching the candle tightly.

Heidi was fast asleep, so Annie crept on tiptoe lest she waken her. She knew she was excited and might be easily disturbed. As she looked at her little sister, she felt proud that she belonged to such a caring family. She knew that Heidi did not understand fully the pain or loss, but as she grew older, she would miss a father figure in the home. She knelt at her bedside and prayed a little prayer for Heidi, Benny and Mama. Heidi did not stir as she climbed into bed beside her.

A Child's Christmas Eve

I hung my stocking on a chair,
knelt and prayed a little prayer;
asking God that Santa would
be safe on his big sleigh;
that he would see the food and drink
I left him near the kitchen sink:
I counted stars, I counted sheep;
What else would make me go to sleep?
Would Santa know that I was seven?
My little brother two?
Perhaps I should have made it plain!
Should I creep down, write and explain?
I crept from under my big quilt,
feeling a little tinge of guilt:
Would Mum be cross?

For unto you is born this day
in the city of David a Saviour,
which is Christ the Lord.
Luke 2 : 11

The house was still, the light was low,
The fire was still a healthy glow:
I tiptoed to the food and drink:
What would I write – I must be quick!

"Dear Santa, I just want to say –
I had a birthday yesterday!
Now I am seven:
My little brother, he is two,
Mama and Papa are twenty - or more!"

I heard a noise, I felt quite numb!
Was it Santa?
My Papa stood there at the door,
He asked what I was looking for:
Then read the note and smiling said,
'My child, you must go back to bed'!
Then he took me on his knee -
Told me of Christ's great love for me;
How Jesus came to Bethlehem,
then died to pardon sinful men:
The reason we have Christmas Day
is just to thank Him for the way
He came to us!
Papa took my hand, and prayed:

"Father, we thank You that You cared
to send Your Son:
He came into this world to show
a little child the way to go!
If we will take Your gift of Love,
Then we shall live with You above!"

My Papa tucked me back in bed:
When he was gone, I prayed and said...

" Forgive me God for I have seen
How mean and selfish I have been!
You loved!
You gave your only Son
And all I want is toys and fun!
Give me the gift of Christ today,
Then help me live for Christ each day!"

God heard my prayer
that Christmas Eve:
Became my Friend: Will never leave!
Will take me to His heavenly Home
when all my work on earth is done!

Annie Had a Restless Night

Annie was restless during the night and wakened before anyone stirred... Without disturbing Heidi, she crept to the window deep in thought. Although it was still dark, the snow glistened as a full moon lit up a white world. The flakes were still falling thick and fast.

"Each flake is different," Annie muttered, as she sat down on the narrow window ledge. Somehow, she had never noticed the different sizes of the snowflakes before. Some of them were blown into the window and melted on the glass. She began to think how different this Christmas Day would be for her family. Life had changed in the Pringle household! There would be no Papa! The tears started to trickle down Annie's cheeks, just like the snowflakes on the window. Then she thought of all the other children who had lost their Papas in the war and offered up a little prayer for them...

"Dear Jesus,
Please help all those children who have no Papa today!

Some of them will already be opening their presents, so give them a very happy time together."
"O God, You made each tiny snowflake different and You made us different. Little Amy Kelly is very different from her brother, Jimmy. He is so strong and she is a sad child since her Papa died. I pray for special help for Amy, dear God, and all the children who have no Papa today.
Amen!"

Opening her eyes, Annie felt a surge of joy! Suddenly, she pictured her Papa in heaven. It was his first Christmas with Jesus and the angels. What would he be doing? Certainly, he would not want his child to be sad at Christmas. She would be thankful for all her happy memories. What comfort it brought as her mind drifted back to the times she had spent with her Papa.

They were special! As she gazed at the falling snow, she found herself drifting back to her earlier childhood. How she cherished every memory of her Papa!

Annie peered through the window in an effort to spot the familiar landmark of the village - the mill's tall chimney! It was usually visible in any part of the village and for miles beyond, but this morning millions of snowflakes blocked it from Annie's searching eyes. She knew it was out there, surrounded by rows of small terraced houses, where happy families would soon be celebrating Christmas Day.

Suddenly, Annie thought of something! I cannot see Papa, but that does not change things. He is in heaven, hidden from us now, but one day it will be clear and we shall see him again!

The Snowflake

Aimless - floating in the breeze,
the gentle snowflake lands with ease

to make her bed on frozen ground -
then nestle down without a sound!
She's unimportant on her own,
but when she's found herself a home,
myriads of gentle flakes of snow
blanket white the world we know!

Aimless – yet with purpose bent,
the snowflake turns her slender back
to bear the strain of other flakes
that merge for winter's birthday cake!
Aimless –now she's lost her name!
Was snowflake's long descent in vain?
Since she lies buried two feet deep –
will wake up in a messy heap!
Then weep her way to watery grave
forgetting all the joy she gave!

Aimless, seems your life at times
until in Christ you purpose find,
when on the grounds of Calvary
you rest your soul, eternally -
then merge into the plan of God,
part of Christ's Body, through His blood
that washed your crimson sin-stained soul
white as the snow in blustery March

Aimless, now you cannot be,
for you will soon your Bridegroom see -
arrayed in white, pure as the snow,
you'll meet the One who loved you so!
Join in the new eternal song -
Worthy, Oh, worthy is the Lamb!

As Annie watched the snowflakes silently fall on the street below, she spotted Captain David Andrews and his son Dave, out for a morning walk. It was difficult to see them through the cloud of falling snowflakes, but she saw the outline of Captain Andrew's arm in a sling and knew it was the army officer and his son out for a brisk walk before breakfast. He was one of the few soldiers from Millvale who returned from the war alive, and that was the first time Annie had seen him out walking. Dave, his son, had a health problem and was medically unfit for the army.

The big Mill along the river

Dave Andrews was a handsome young bachelor and everyone in Millvale knew there was a romance brewing between Dave and Jenny. Annie watched her two neighbours disappear through the snow. She knew the path they would take, over the footbridge and along the far side of the river. Papa often took the family for a walk on the same path. A memory shot into her mind.

One day they met Billy, the village bully, with his dog. The dog was not trained, and very disobedient, for he jumped on Heidi and pulled her into the river; then disappeared into the bushes. Billy ran after him while Papa helped Heidi up the river bank. The water dripped from her clothes and she was very frightened, so Mama picked Heidi up in her arms to reassure her, and carried her home for a change of clothes. We met her on the bridge on the way back, but Billy and his dog had disappeared! Annie thought Papa was very patient, for he never told Billy's father, and said Billy would mature and change when he was older.

Annie struggled with her emotions. Seeing Captain Andrews, made her wonder if Papa had been injured before he died, but she dare not dwell on that and quickly reminded herself that Papa was 'Safe in the Arms of Jesus', and she would recall her happy memories of him.

The highlight of the last year of her Papa's life was the day he took her to the big city. Annie recalled her father lifting her in his strong arms and telling her how hard Mama's father and mother had to work in the mill to feed the family. Papa had said that if there was no food the children would have to go into the 'workhouse' or 'the poorhouse' as some people called it. When he was a little boy, some of his playmates had to go into the poorhouse and he had never seen them again or heard about them. His workmates talked about some from the village who had to go into the workhouse because their parents had no money to feed them.

Mr. Pringle had promised Annie he would take her to the big city. Because she felt sorry for the poor children whose parents could not provide food and clothes for them, she asked her Papa to take her to the workhouse. Just before her birthday, Mama and Papa told her that her special birthday present was going to be a train journey to the city and a visit to the workhouse.

Still gazing at the falling snow, Annie recalled how her father had kept his promise.

It was her first train journey. There was the build up of excitement as she planned for the day. Her friends at school had told the teacher.

The day before the trip, Miss Diane asked Annie to note all the interesting things and then she could tell them about it at school.

Annie was reluctant, but she agreed. It made her a little nervous as she thought of standing up in front of all her friends: she also felt sad that they were not able to go and see the city too. Few of them had ever been to the city for only the wealthy and the hard working men went to the city on business or to the market. Most of the families in Millvale could not afford a day out, nor take the time for such a luxury.

If it would help the pupils to understand more about their own country, Annie felt she should share her experience with them.

Miss Diane had told the class about the workhouse in a history lesson, so everyone was interested in Annie's trip to the city. In the afternoon prior to Annie's trip, Miss Diane reminded the children and wished Annie a wonderful day.

"Don't forget to take notes," Miss Diane said, "We all want to learn more about our city, Annie, so we will depend on you to help us glean more information about our past."

Rachel Kelly, the top pupil in her class, asked her so many questions, that Annie felt embarrassed! She did not have the answers but promised to ask Papa on the day. Her mind was so full she wondered how she would remember it all, but Papa knew everything: he would help her prepare for her talk in school.

Mama had to look after the other two children and cook the evening meal. Papa had saved for a long time to be able to afford the trip.

Such was the excitement it was difficult to sleep the night before.

Mama wakened Annie and had two packed lunches prepared. She too was excited for she knew it was the greatest day in Annie's life. It would never be forgotten!

They got to the station and Papa bought the tickets. Because Annie was watching the ticket collector with his black uniform and shining buttons, she did not see if her Papa had to pay for her, but she thought she may have travelled free. The ticket collector wore a peak cap that had a shining badge on the front and a band around the rim. When they got onto the platform, there was another man in uniform carrying a flag and a whistle. He was so busy lifting parcels and answering questions from passengers that he did not see that Annie's eyes were riveted on him.

There was a lot of noise as doors banged and people called to each other, but soon we were all on the train and slowly it chugged out of the station with everybody chatting happily in the carriage. Sitting beside Papa, Annie felt like a queen as she relaxed on the lovely velvet seat beside the window.

That first train journey was so special! She sat quietly at first looking out of the window.

"We are going over a bridge Papa! Look below, there is a river, and people under the other bridge on the narrow road below."

"Are they going to work Papa?" asked Annie inquisitively.

"It could be furniture making, Annie. I know there is a village not very far away from here where they make furniture."

"If you look carefully, you will soon see the chimney of a factory. It is a jam factory! You may see the workers going to work."

Within what seemed like seconds to Annie, she did see the big chimney, just like the one in her own village.

"Look Papa! I see it! Look at the people going to work!"

Stonebridge, Co. Armagh.

It was gone in a flash...

"Faster than fairies, faster than witches
Bridges and houses, hedges and ditches!"

After the excitement of seeing so much that was new to her, Annie watched the houses and hedges flash past, then commented to her Papa...

"Now I know why Miss Diane said the train was the greatest invention of our time."

Annie asked her papa about trains and how people travelled long ago.

When Papa saw that Annie was interested in inventions, he talked about the first carts for carrying goods. They were 'sleigh-carts', like the sleighs used on the icy village hill in Millvale, but instead of a flat base, a small box was built on top to carry goods. These carts were pulled by hand through the country. Because the narrow roads were of mud, they glided smoothly when it was snowing or raining.

Some time later, Annie's father told her, somebody invented wheels for the carts. This was much better and carts were built much larger with two shafts so that horses could pull them. The next invention was the motor car. Annie was able to understand how ideas became inventions as Papa explained the history of transport.

*"The train was the greatest invention," Papa said with a sense of pride!

*   In 1903 the airplane was invented. Its significance was not fully recognized until after the First World War. It was two Ohio brothers who finally fulfilled their dream and invented the first 'flying machine'. At Kitty Hawk, North Carolina, Orville and Wilbur Wright made the first powered flight. Although the first flight covered less distance than the wingspan of a jumbo jet, it began a revolution in transport. In 1909, six years after the Wright brothers built the first 'flying machine' in America, Henry Ferguson became famous by flying the first 'flying machine' in Ireland.

"Bicycles must be an invention too, Papa," said Annie thoughtfully.

"The first bicycle was the 'Hobby-horse', then the 'Penny-farthing'." Although Annie had never seen a picture of the Penny-farthing bicycle, her father painted a clear image of a frame with a huge wheel at the front and a tiny one at the back. It was a major invention by a French man, Pierre Michaux and his son, Ernest.

The Penny Farthing Bicycle.

"It was discovered that a frame with two wheels, two pedals with a connecting chain, a saddle and a manual control steered by hand, could move forward at greater speed than walking, if balanced with leg movement operating the pedals."

"Mind you Papa! I would be very happy if I had a bicycle!" Annie and Papa looked at each other and smiled!

"Was the bicycle invented before the train?"

He did not have time to answer her question for the train jerked and came to a standstill.

"We have reached the city Papa. The train has stopped!"

Soon the doors opened and everyone headed for the exit. Everybody was moving quickly - possibly afraid they would have been taken to the next station.

Papa gripped Annie's hand tightly as they squeezed towards the open door. They were hemmed in by dozens of bodies and deafened by the boisterous chatter of small children and their parents. Annie's excitement knew no bounds as she stepped onto the platform.

On the platform she watched the man in the uniform walk up and down closing doors. He had a whistle in his hand, like the one her teacher used in the playground at school. He then waved a flag and blew the whistle. The train chugged out of the station. It let off steam, making a loud noise as it disappeared from view.

There were so many questions Annie wanted to ask Papa about the train and the men in the black suits with shining buttons and peak caps, but they had to move on with the other passengers and show their tickets to a man in the same uniform.

When they left the station, Annie saw a big church.

"I have never seen such a big church Papa. Could we go into it?" Annie asked.

"That is a cathedral. Another day I will bring you back to visit the cathedral, but we must go directly to the workhouse in order to return to the station in time to catch the last train home."

Armagh Cathedral

Typical market stall

A Day in The City

People were waiting outside the train station. There were ponies and traps parked along one side of the street. Passengers mounted the traps with the help of a footman. The ladies looked elegant in their feathered hats and long flowing gowns! Because Annie had been so lost in the train journey and the arrival at the railway station, she had not noticed the posh ladies. Of course they may have been in another part of the train. Some of the men standing by the ponies were dressed in

Annie at the Train Station

black coats with a long tail at the back. They wore big tall hats and white gloves. Annie could see her face reflected on their shoes, they were so shiny.

Other passengers left with simple hand - made sacks slung over their backs. There was nobody to meet them and they disappeared quickly. Annie wondered if they had a good home and people to love and care for them. Even girls and boys her age left with large sacks on their backs and many of them with no shoes. Around the street there were a few children begging for money, but they did not persist. Their clothes looked ragged, their hair unkempt, and their sad faces haunted Annie for weeks.

The streets of the city were cobblestone. Neat rows of terraced houses lined the long street leading from the station to the city centre. After walking a short distance, Papa took Annie by the hand and kept her close to him. There seemed to be millions of people around, as they turned a corner and went down a steep hill. Annie's father had explained that there was a big Farmer's Market – for that reason there were more people than normal. Farmers passed with animals they had bought: there were horses and carts, ponies and traps, wheelbarrows full of plants and women with cabbages and carrots stacked at their children's feet in the prams. They were chatting merrily to each other and seemed to be enjoying their day out.

At the bottom of a hill, there was a large green on the right. Men dressed in white shirts, trousers and shoes, played with a small ball and a long, thin bat. There were women and children walking leisurely along the path and others were seated watching the game. They looked like the ladies Annie saw earlier at the station - obviously they were the elite of the city!

"Those ladies look very elegant!" said Annie. "They must have servants at home to do the work!"

She was fascinated by their gowns and gestures, as they flaunted their dress with hand gestures to display their long fingers, covered with white, silk gloves.

Annie was beginning to get tired. "Have we far to go now Papa?" she said as they climbed the next hill and passed a school. Then, as they were about to turn the corner to climb the last hill to the workhouse, Annie swung round and gasped at the view.

"Papa! Look at the city! There's the cathedral! What an amazing view! I never imagined it would be so beautiful!"

She held her breath as she looked in every direction. Neither spoke for what seemed an eternity. Papa watched Annie's face intently for he had never seen Annie lost for words, nor had he ever seen her so excited. Eventually she broke the silence by thanking Papa for giving her such a wonderful birthday present.

"It is a memory I will always treasure, Papa! Thank you so much for keeping your promise! You are the world's best Papa!"

Papa hid his emotion, but Annie knew he was pleased to see her so happy. He too was happy to be able to spend time with his daughter.

Within a short time they were at the *workhouse. It was a well kept, grey, stone building. Annie tried to imagine what it must have been like for those children who had no food to go to live away from their Mamas and Papas with people who were not always kind to them.

It seemed a long time from they had eaten, but she knew that the end was in sight: soon she would be on a tour of the workhouse.

At the gate she peeped through the iron bars and saw an old man in the courtyard. He looked confused. Annie noticed two large patches on his trousers and wondered if his wife was with him and if she had sewn the patches on his trousers, like Mama did for Papa.

Mr. Pringle knew the residents would be having their mid-day meal so he suggested that they eat their packed lunches. They walked

Old man with patches on his trousers.

beyond the entrance and found a patch of grassland. Annie gave a sigh of relief as she pulled off her shoes and stretched out on the grass. Papa brought out the lunches and bottles of milk that Mama had prepared for them. It was a beautiful, sunny day, so it felt like a picnic outing.

"What a pity Mama, Heidi and Benny are not with us Papa!"

"Benny is too small and Heidi is not old enough to understand the pain and sadness in the world, Annie. That's the reason I waited until you were almost twelve years old. Soon you will be entering your teens and girls soon move from childhood to adolescence when they experience new emotions and are exposed to a big world full of new and interesting experiences. All too soon you will become an adult and leave childhood forever – that is until you get married and have children of your own. Then you start to relive your own childhood and enjoy your children's tender age. Always remember that Annie!"

"Are all Papas so wise?" quizzed Annie.

Papa smiled, but did not comment.

"It's time to go Annie! Finish your milk, you need calcium for those tired bones!"

Within minutes they were back at the gate. The old man with patches on his trousers, was standing looking through the bars. He seemed to be expecting someone.

Papa and Annie were taken to the office by a skinny little man, who looked like one of the poor men sweeping the yard. Annie got a new lease of life and forgot about her tired feet as the large, heavy, wooden door opened and father and daughter began their tour. She noted the cobblestone floor and bare stone walls of the awesome building. Two twelve year old girls were down on their knees washing the floor as they were introduced to a portly woman with a stern look of authority. She did smile when the two visitors were introduced to her.

"Call me Miss Winnie," she said, as she started to walk further along the corridor away from the pathetic gaze of the two poorly clad children.

"Do those children have any parents, Miss Winnie?" Annie asked.

"Yes, but their parents have no money to..."

Before Miss Winnie could finish answering the question, there was a loud bang! A door opened and a thirteen year old boy fell to the floor in front of them! A burly big fellow, who was unaware that Miss Winnie was showing guests around, stood over the boy on the floor with his fists clenched.

"Get up," he shouted! "You're a coward! Come on, let's fight it out!"

Annie and her Papa were face to face with a big fight! But Miss Winnie was soon in control.

"Billy Giles, stop this fight immediately! Come with me, both of you!"

Papa and Annie knew they would have to wait. One of the girls washing the floor was called and they were left with a shy Mary Blevins.

Mary was the same age as Annie, but it was obvious she was a lonely girl who was the victim of hardship.

Conversation with Mary was difficult. Annie wanted to befriend the poor unfortunate girl.

"Do you have brothers and sisters, Mary?"

"Yes, that's my brother who has gone with Miss Winnie."

Without lifting her eyes, Mary buried her face in her apron and sobbed. Annie put her arm around her and gave Mary her hankie.

"I know Billy, the bully, will be punished, but he is always picking a fight with other boys. This time it's my brother, Pete.

"Please, will your Papa ask Miss Winnie to move Pete to another bedroom? It's not fair, that he has to be with that bad boy!"

Miss Winnie returned and Mary went back to her job. A warden was with Billy to collect his few belongings to move him to another room. Miss Winnie then gave her undivided attention to her guests. She explained that the great potato famine in Ireland left many people starving, and even after a lapse of many years, there was still a lot of poverty.

"The government decided to help such families and a wealthy man built the workhouse in 1860.

"Business men and farmers from Co Armagh bring gifts of apples, bread and poultry to help us feed the poor," Miss Winnie said.

"How kind of them," Annie replied.

"True! But many more could help us, but they only think of a healthy bank balance. As long as they have food for their family and can save for the future, that's all that matters. It would seem the more you have the more you want!" She did not hesitate to give her opinion.

Annie thought it was sad that the apple growers and farmers didn't support Miss Winnie and the workhouse. She knew from her lessons at school that a lot of apples were grown within a few miles of the city. When she visited Uncle Ben on the farm, he told her about the orchards and the fruit export trade from the county. Uncle Ben told lots of interesting things about planting and producing good apples. He called the big green cooking apples; 'Bramley', and every year he brought big sacks of the apples for Mama to cook for the family. Annie thought that farmers should bring sacks of apples to Miss Winnie for the residents at the workhouse.

As Annie and Papa went down the corridor, they were shown the dorms where the children slept. They were clean and tidy and it gave Miss Winnie great pleasure to explain that those who lived in the workhouse did chores to earn their keep.

"This gives them a sense of dignity," she said, "and teaches them to care for property. Hopefully, one day they will be free to leave and fend for themselves! Our job brings satisfaction when we see people develop and hopefully face a better future."

"Come now there is a cup of hot chocolate ready for you. Mr. Arnold is waiting in the kitchen to take you to see his garden. He takes great pride in growing the vegetables, so make sure you give him positive comments, Mr. Pringle! Although it is early, there is a lot of work to be done to till the soil in preparation for the sowing."

Miss Winnie laughed heartily, which took Annie by surprise, for she thought she was a very stern woman. She realized that Miss Winnie was a strong character who had developed a side to her character that might not have been there prior to her appointment as matron. After Papa had thanked her, Annie wanted to give her a hug in appreciation of her good work, but thought it would be inappropriate and refrained. Instead, she gave her a warm handshake and thanked her for her help and for the milky chocolate drink.

As Miss Winnie finished her tour of the building, a strong, broad-shouldered man in dungarees, met them at the exit. Without an introduction, he moved forward to carry out his instructions from Miss Winnie.

"Follow me!" he said without looking at either Papa or Annie. He did not seem to want a friendly conversation, so the two visitors followed as instructed.

"I will take you around the grounds. You will see how we grow many of our own vegetables and fruit. The orchard is not in bloom at this time of the year. We are inspecting the trees to see if there is any sign of disease. They can easily get 'black spot', which would be a disaster. I am glad to say the trees are healthy and we should have a good crop of cooking and eating apples."

Residents were as busy as bees and accelerated their pace when we appeared! All ages were involved. Children working beside grown ups looked at them inquisitively, obviously wondering why they were walking through the garden with Mr. Arnold.

Annie spoke to the children and hoped they were happy at their work. Mr Pringle asked Mr. Arnold lots of questions about the produce.

"Are you able to sell any surplus at the local market and make some money for other essential food produce?" he enquired.

"No," replied Mr. Arnold.

"When we feed the residents, there is no food left and we would really need more help from the government to feed these poor people!"

Annie felt sad as she listened to the two men talking about the little children and their parents. She wished she could do something to help, but she knew Mama and Papa could not afford anything from their already low income.

"Perhaps some day, things will get better," she whispered to her father.

Mr. Arnold's attitude changed during their walk around the garden. Mr. Pringle's interest in his produce was the breaking point.

"At least someone appreciates my hard work in this garden! Usually all I get are complaints from the residents that they have to work too hard, or from Miss Winnie that I am late bringing in the potatoes and vegetables for the cooks. At least someone appreciates my hard work!"

He confessed to his visitors that he often felt it was a 'thankless' job that neither the staff nor the residents appreciated.

"You are doing a good job, Mr. Arnold," commented Annie. "Who else would provide potatoes, vegetables and fruit for those poor unfortunate people?"

Mr. Arnold was surprised at the young girl's frankness. His dour expression changed to one of sincere appreciation, as he took his hand from his pocket and gave Annie a farthing.

"Thank you so much Mr. Arnold. It is very kind of you. Papa and I want you to know we are grateful for your hard work to feed these poor people."

Just as they were leaving the garden, a robin started to sing.

"I think the robin appreciates your work in the garden too, Mr. Arnold! Listen to him singing. He is saying 'thank you'!"

Papa and Mr. Arnold laughed!

"Annie has a point!" was Papa's comment.

The old man with the patches on his trousers was back at the gate. Annie wished she could give him something but knew Mr. Arnold would be upset if she gave him the farthing. She took his old wrinkled hand in both her smooth gentle hands as she said 'Goodbye!'

"I hope the future will be brighter for you! May God help you!" The old man's confused expression slowly changed and his eyes brightened as Annie spoke to him. Papa asked him if he had a wife and family, to which he replied,

"I don't know anything about my wife and boys. I wish you could find my youngest son, Fred."

Mr. Pringle asked Arnold if he knew where his son lived, only to discover that he lived in Millvale. When Mr. Pringle made further enquiries he discovered that old man Herron's youngest son worked in the mill and lived with his wife and family in the village. One day at the * 'cocoa break' Mr. Pringle had chatted to Fred Herron about his father, who told him he wandered off after a row with his mother and never returned. Fred concluded his father was dead, as did everyone in Millvale. His two older sons had gone to live in another part of Ireland and had not communicated with Fred. Mr. Pringle was able to tell the old man about his son and assured him he would give him the good news that his father was still alive.

"Is my wife Jane alive?" He spoke softly, as he raised his head hopefully to await Mr. Pringle's reply. Sadly he heard the news that she had died five years previously. The old man's eyes filled with tears.

"She was a good woman, but times were hard and I was broke. I could not provide for my family!"

He sobbed bitterly as he confessed his folly. He confirmed to Mr. Pringle what Fred had told him about his father - after a row with his wife, he had left home and never returned. The old man found it difficult to talk to them, as he told them how he found his way to the city where he became a pauper. One day a man offered to buy him a drink and took him to a pub – that was the beginning of his sad ending! He was found lying drunk outside a bar and was taken to the workhouse. He had never been outside the big gate again. The old man wiped his tears with the sleeve of his coat. Annie turned away. She had heard one of the most tragic stories ever and was deeply moved. Even Mr. Arnold found the story touch his heart strings for he took the old man by the arm assuring him that he would be cared for: that his son would soon come to see him.

Arnold left them at the big gate. Papa thanked him for his helpfulness, but Annie was so sad leaving the old man that she could not speak: she waved to the two figures disappearing across the courtyard. Then, as if a new surge of strength filled her body, she shouted after the two men -

"Mr. Herron, Papa will tell your son Fred at the mill. Don't worry he will soon know where you are and it will not be long before he is here to visit you. Please believe me - my Papa always keeps his promises!"

Descending the hill, Papa placed his arm on Annie's shoulder and affectionately patted her. He did not need to say anything for Annie knew they both would not rest until Fred Herron found his Papa and the old man at the workhouse with two patches on his trousers, found his son.

- Most weaving factories provided a welcome mug of cocoa for their workers in the mid-morning.

- The workhouse was built by a legacy designated for that purpose by Charles Shields in 1860.

The Homeward Journey

The cricket match was over and there were few people on the green, apart from a few children kicking a small football at the far end.

"They have gone home for their evening meal. Come Annie, we must quicken our pace to get back to the station for the train."

At the big courthouse, opposite the green, there were soldiers standing in uniform. They watched us as we mounted the hill and turned the corner to the station. Annie had read about soldiers in school and had seen them pass through the village, but had never been so close to them. She felt afraid and was glad her Papa was there to reassure her.

"War clouds were gathering over Europe," Miss Diane, the school teacher had told the class.

"Already, British soldiers are arriving in Ireland. They are here to protect us," Miss Diane had told her pupils.

"Don't be afraid of them. They are your friends!"

Annie was glad she remembered what Miss Diane had said.

She did feel frightened when she saw the men in uniform. They carried guns.

Back at the station, people had gathered for the last train. As they went through the door, a weary five or six year old boy tugged at his mother's dress and pleaded with her to carry him. The mother looked ill and her husband was laden with heavy bags of potatoes and wood. Mr. Pringle lifted the boy and carried him to the train. The little lad was too tired to cry and did not seem to be frightened. As soon as they were on the train, he snuggled up beside his mother and was soon fast asleep; the man on the opposite side of them had a small piglet beside him in a sack. The piglet was frightened and struggled to get out, but the farmer had tied the sack with a piece of string, and there was no escape for the little snorting animal. Papa had told Annie to secure seats on the opposite side of the train for the homeward journey. Despite people pushing her to get aboard the train, she managed to edge her way through the crowd and Papa joined her at the window.

Soon the whistle blew and the train chugged along the track.

Suddenly, Annie spotted a castle.

Richhill Castle

"Look Papa! I see a castle!"

Papa missed it, but Annie was sure she saw a castle as the train whizzed past. Within seconds they crossed the bridge, Annie could see some children playing at the river's edge.

"What are they doing Papa?" she asked inquisitively.

"They are catching eels or small 'sticklies' (sticklebacks)," said Papa.

"Look Papa, quickly! One boy is in a bath tub and is moving forward with two large pieces of wood. They are having such fun! Perhaps we could do that on the river in Millvale!"

Mr. Pringle laughed as he caught sight of an old man listening to their conversation and seemed amused at the child's innocence!

Papa had told Annie to remind him to tell her about the train crash on the Newry line. He did not want to tell her as they began their journey home, in case she would be frightened on the train.

Trains were the greatest invention

When they were near their destination, Mr. Pringle became sombre as he told Annie about the fateful train journey on the Newry line. "A lot of children and their mothers were travelling to the seaside on their

Sunday school trip, when the driver made a mistake and the train crashed into another train coming in the opposite direction.

"There are some very sad homes in the city today because of the disaster: carriages went off the rail and crashed down a grassy embankment. Many of the Mother's and children were killed and more than four hundred were injured."

"It is something that will never be forgotten!" said Mr. Pringle with a tone of sadness in his voice.

The rest of the journey became a blur because Annie had seen so much and learned so much, she was tired in mind and body. When she went through the front door, all she wanted was her comfortable bed, though she did eat with relish her mother's good food. She was hungry, but her story would have to wait for another day.

As she climbed into bed, she glanced at Heidi who was in dreamland, then put her weary head on the pillow and was fast asleep in a few minutes.

Fast asleep!

Teddy in the Fire by Jennifer Hampton

The Candle by Chloe Metcalf (age 9)

The Robin by Jill Morrow (age 9)

Three Stockings by Meghan Byrnes (age 13)

The Spirit of Giving by Megan Lyttle (age 13)

Old Railway Signal Box still in use

Old wheel from Scutch Mill

Apples from the farm

Annie deep in thought

Bruno meets his new neighbours

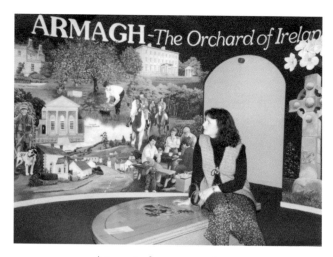

A trip into the past in comfort

A new day dawns in Ireland

A Nightmare

"Miss Winnie! Miss Winnie! Please come quickly! Billy, the bully is fighting with a boy! He has punched him on the eye and he is bleeding very badly. Miss Winnie, the poor boy is badly hurt. Do come and rescue him!"

Annie woke crying! She had dreamt about Billy the bully at the workhouse and woke up stiff with fright.

Papa rushed to her bedside!

"You are alright Annie! You are home in Millvale with Mama and Papa. Heidi and Benny are having their breakfast. Come and join the family. We are waiting for you to come and tell the others about your trip yesterday!"

Annie laughed heartily!

"Oh, Papa, I am so glad I woke out of the dreadful nightmare! There was blood everywhere. That wicked boy was beating up a smaller boy in the workhouse – and it wasn't Mary Blevins' brother, Pete! It was a much smaller boy with curly hair and a very sad face!"

"Come! Come Annie! You must forget about Billy, the bully. Miss Winnie and her staff will sort out the problem. Billy will leave the workhouse a different boy. Miss Winnie knows how to deal with bullies!"

Mama was pleased for Annie! As she joined the family at the breakfast table next morning, there was lots to tell, so Papa and Annie kept talking while Mama, Heidi and Benny ate their breakfast. Mama had to take the plates of cold porridge and reheat them for Papa and Annie. Heidi and Benny were allowed to leave the table.

Annie helped Mama to wash up and Papa brought the firewood in for the day. Annie got a pencil and notebook to write down everything for her talk at school. It was important to get Papa's help while the trip was still fresh in his mind.

An hour later, the Begley children from next door arrived, then some of her school friends knocked on the door. Even the star pupil in her class, Beverly Green, arrived to find out from Annie all she had gleaned from her trip.

It seemed everyone knew Annie Pringle had been to the big city! Of course Annie was pleased to see all her friends and eagerly related the events of the previous day.

"Have you written everything down Annie?"asked Beverly.

"I am really looking forward to hearing all about your trip. Perhaps some day, I will be able to go and learn more about our city," she sighed, wistfully!

Annie knew that would be very difficult for Beverly, as her father had very poor health and was seldom able to work.

"Oh Beverly," said Annie, "I know you would really enjoy it, and you would be able to report to the class every detail of what you saw! I just hope I will be able to remember it all, but Papa knows everything and he will remind me of the things I forget. Beverly, there are times when I wish I was as clever as you!"

Beverly Green blushed and felt quite embarrassed. Annie was sorry she had made the statement to cause Beverly such embarrassment, but everyone in the village knew that Beverly was the 'brain box' of Millvale. She was always first in the class!

"By the way," broke in Bessie Begley – "I forgot to congratulate you on your success again in the Christmas exams! Well done, Bev! You deserved it for you worked so hard all year!"

Annie had a vivid imagination and an amazing memory. She was able to recall all the details. She got quite excited relating the details of her nightmare. The girls were highly amused and broke into fits of laughter.

"You would have been frightened too," laughed Annie!

Jack Pringle told Annie that Mr. Pepper's had a
Grandfather clock in his hall

Sadness and Surprises

The clock striking six o'clock wakened Annie from her day-dreams. "Christmas Day!" breathed Annie. Shaking herself, she felt a new strength.

Her memories had helped her cope with her grief. She sensed a release from the great pain that had given her a sleepless night and braced herself to be able to help Mama face her grief.

Everyone was still fast asleep, so she crept on tip-toe to the living room. She could hear laughter from the Begley children next door. They were already up and had started the Christmas celebrations.

Annie was so pleased to hear them laughing because she knew of their sorrow in losing little Toby. Then she discovered the reason for their happiness.

"Bow-wow! Bow-wow!" echoed through the wall that separated their living rooms. It was the sharp piercing bark of a puppy.

Santa Claus had brought the Begley family a new puppy. What breed of dog was it? What would it be called? Annie found herself deciding on a name for the new Begley puppy. Certainly she would make suggestions. But perhaps they would already have decided! It would have to be different from Teddybear Toby – there could only be one 'Toby', Annie concluded! Goldie would be suitable if it were a Golden Labrador!

She would have to wait. Annie knew she would know later when Joey, Bessie and Jonnie Begley would bring their new puppy to meet the Pringle neighbours.

Annie was disturbed by the shouts of Heidi and Benny. Suddenly she had to switch to the celebrations of Christmas Day.

Both Heidi and Benny grabbed their Christmas stocking and emptied out the contents on the rug. They gazed at them in dismay!

"I onwy got a wapple and a sweetie," sighed Benny miserably.

"Perhaps Father Christmas doesn't like us," Heidi lamented.

Mrs Pringle turned to Annie, her eyes full of tears. There was a great lump in her throat.

"Oh, Annie, the poor darlins." I only wish I could have given them more but our finances simply couldn't stretch any further.

"Never mind Mama," said Annie, consolingly. Look! it's snowing outside, and...LOOK!...Mama, LOOK!"

She turned round and peered outside. Then she drew back catching her breath.

"I ... I don't believe it Annie. I must be dreaming."

"Quickly child, fetch my coat...Hurry!"

Annie rushed to her mother's room and came scurrying back with her coat. Mrs. Pringle quickly pulled on her coat and draped a scarf over her head, and Mother and daughter hurried outside.

Phew! It was cold! But their excitement knew no bounds.

Annie didn't feel the cold although the snow was still falling thick and fast as they plodded over to the garden fence.

Sure enough, propped against the wooden gate was a sack with a Christmas card attached. Annie pulled it off and read...

To the Pringle Family! Happy Christmas!'

Annie peeped inside - there were parcels wrapped in brightly coloured paper. Mrs Pringle gasped! Mother and daughter stood in silence gazing out through the snow. There was nobody to be seen. Who left the presents? Would they ever know? Mrs. Pringle opened the gate and called out into the silence...

"Is there anybody out there?" There was no reply! Then the church bells began to peel out and Mrs Pringle said,

"Annie, we must hide the presents. Fetch Heidi and Benny. We're going to church."

Mrs. Pringle and her family joined the villagers making their way to church. It was a sad day for the many families who had lost a father or son at war. The first person they met was Mrs. Pringle's good friend Gretta, who had shed many tears with her during the past months. Gretta Dawson had also lost her husband in the war, so both women shared a deep sorrow. When news of John's death reached Gretta, she turned to Mrs. Pringle for comfort for she knew she would understand her loss. Her two small daughters were too young to understand, so they joined Benny sliding on the ice.

"Come! Come children! We must hurry along to church," said Gretta as she gained her composure. Benny slipped but fortunately was not hurt. As the family stepped from the slippery street into the warmth of the old church, the organist was playing Annie's best-loved carol, *'Away in a Manger...'*

Annie found herself humming the tune as she followed her mother to the family pew. The Pringle family took their seats behind Frank Murphy and his four boys, Danny, Phil, Pete and Gerry.

"This must be a sad Christmas for the Murphy family," Annie whispered in her mother's ear.

"Yes, Annie, say a little prayer for them."

Silently, Annie prayed...

"Dear God:

Mary Murphy went to be with you in heaven a few months ago. Poor Frank, Dan, Phil, Pete and Gerry had no Mama this morning as they opened their Christmas presents and when they go home from church they will have no Mama to serve their Christmas dinner. Please help them and give them a happy Christmas. Help them to know that their Mama is happy with you and will spend her first Christmas in heaven."

"Please tell Mary Murphy that we miss her in church today, but Frank and the boys look happy enough."

Before Annie could say 'Amen,' Jane Burns, who was sitting in the pew behind her, poked her in the back to show her the book she got in her Christmas stocking. Annie glanced round and peeped at the title of the book. She knew Jane would let her read it when they started back to school in the New Year.

There were special items for the children, some of whom had brought their toys to church. Mr. Robert James, the Sunday school teacher, was in charge of the Christmas morning programme, and as soon as he announced the first carol, there was quietness. The only sound was the organ music and the sound of rustling paper as parents found the page for their children. Parents and children sang heartily...

See Amid the Winter's Snow

See Amid the Winter's snow,
Born for us on earth below;
See the tender Lamb appears,
Promised from eternal years:

Hail thou ever-blessed morn!
Hail redemption's happy dawn!
Sing through all Jerusalem,
'Christ is born in Bethlehem!

Lo! Within a manger lies
He who built the starry skies,
 He who, throned in height sublime,
Sits amid the cherubim!

Say, ye holy shepherds, say
What your joyful news to-day;
Wherefore have ye left your sheep
On the lonely mountain steep?

"As we watched at dead of night
Lo, we saw a wondrous light:
Angels singing 'Peace on earth'
Told us of the Saviour's birth!

Sacred infant, all Divine,
What a tender love was Thine,
Thus to come from highest bliss
Down to such a world as this!

Teach, O teach us holy Child,
By Thy face so meek and mild,
Teach us to resemble Thee
In Thy sweet humility!   *[Edward Caswall, 1814 -1878]*

When a group of six children sang their special song, 'God's Special Gift', Annie left her seat and walked bravely to the front. She was nervous, but nobody knew how she felt. She read the Christmas story from 'Luke 2: 1 – 20. It was perfect! Not a single mistake!

"And it came to pass in those days, that there was a decree from Caesar Augustus, that all the world should be taxed.
(And this taxing was first made when Cyrenius was governor of Syria.)
And all went to be taxed, every one into his own city.
And Joseph also went up from Galilee, out of the city of Nazareth, into Judea, unto the city of David, which is called Bethlehem; (because he was of the house and lineage of David:)
To be taxed with Mary his espoused wife, being great with child.
And so it was, that, while they were there, the days were accomplished that she should be delivered.
And she brought forth her first born son, and wrapped him in swaddling clothes, and laid him in a manger; because there was no room for them in the inn.
And there were in the same country shepherds abiding in the fields, keeping watch over their flocks by night.

And, lo, the angel of the Lord came upon them, and the glory of the Lord shone round about them: and they were sore afraid.

And the angel said unto them, Fear not: for, behold, I bring you good tidings of great joy, which shall be to all people.

For unto you is born this day in the city of David a Saviour, which is Christ the Lord.

And this shall be a sign unto you; Ye shall find the babe wrapped in swaddling clothes, lying in a manger.

And suddenly there was with the angel a multitude of the heavenly host praising God and saying,

Glory to God in the highest, and on earth peace, good will toward men.

And it came to pass, as the angels were gone away from them into heaven, the shepherds said one to another, Let us now go even unto Bethlehem, and see this thing which is come to pass, which the Lord has made known unto us.

And they came with haste, and found Mary, and Joseph, and the babe lying in a manger.

And when they had seen it, they made known the saying which was told them concerning this child.

And all they that heard it wondered at those things which were told them by the shepherds.

But Mary kept all these things, and pondered them in her heart.

And the shepherds returned, glorifying and praising God for all the things that they had heard and seen, as it was told unto them."

*(version in use at this period in history – a more recent version can be found at the end of the book)

"I'm so proud of you Annie," whispered Mrs. Pringle when Annie rejoined the family. Everyone stood and recited...**'The Lord's Prayer'.**

"Our Father which art in heaven, hallowed be Thy name. Thy kingdom come, Thy will be done on earth as it is in heaven. Give us this day our daily bread and forgive us our trespasses, as we forgive them who trespass against us. And lead us not into temptation, but deliver us from evil: for Thine is the kingdom, the power and the glory: for ever and ever.

Amen."

After the prayer, the youth leader prayed for those who had lost a family member in the war. He prayed for the wives, the children in the church who had bravely come to worship. Then he prayed for the sick and for those who were sad and lonely at Christmas. When everyone had settled down in their seats, the youth leader asked Miss Diane, the local schoolteacher, to come and talk to the children. All the children loved Miss Diane. She was a good teacher and took a special interest in children from poor families. She knew how difficult it was for parents to educate their children, while at the same time clothe and feed them. When there was sickness in their homes, Miss Diane always called to see if she could help: she baked soda farls and wheaten bannocks and never went to visit empty handed. When Miss Diane went to the front of the church, she wished them a very Happy Christmas – everyone responded with a welcoming smile! There was total silence as she spoke. Even the tiny tots forgot about their Christmas presents and listened carefully.

"If I could give you a present this morning that would make you really happy and contented, what would it be?" The children gave various answers – teddies, footballs, a train, a fire engine...

"Sometimes we look at what others have and think this would make us happy. I have a list of things I would like to show you. "Miss Diane pulled out a very long sheet of white paper on which she had written her 'wants'...

"MY LIST – first, new 'gutties' for games at school; a handbag; a bicycle; a skirt; 'wellies' for the garden and the list went on and on! I could add to the list!

"I might think that the things on my list would make me really happy! Many of us think that by getting things, it would make us happy. Would they really make us happy?

"The Lord Jesus told a story about a foolish farmer who had lots of barns. He grew more crops and decided he would pull down his barns and build even bigger ones. He was more interested in getting more for himself than in following the Lord Jesus. The Lord Jesus called him 'a fool' and He warned us against being greedy and for wanting what others have. True happiness doesn't come from having things.

"How then can we be truly happy or contented?

"BE A FOLLOWER OF THE LORD JESUS CHRIST. He is the most important person we can follow. Toys can be broken, things can be lost but the Lord Jesus Christ will always be there for us. We need to tell Him we are sorry for all the wrong things we have done and ask Him to be our Saviour and come into our lives, If we come to Him in prayer and ask Him to be our Saviour, He will do it! When we do this, we go into the future knowing that He is with us. Then, boys and girls, He will be with us for the rest of our lives and take us to heaven when we die.

"Even if bad things happen to us in the New Year or anytime in the future, the Lord Jesus has promised never to leave us or forsake us, and He will keep His promise. He loves us and has a special plan for our lives. It does not mean that life will always be easy, but it does mean that He will be with us in the bad times as well as in the good times.

"Be content with what you have, because true happiness and contentment comes from being a follower of the Lord Jesus Christ."

"What was the best gift you received this morning?" asked the youth leader.

After a few seconds, hands shot up everywhere. Heidi and Benny didn't put their hands up, for they were not happy about their presents. It was Jimmy Liggett who had his hand up first.

"I got the best gift ever. A bright red fire engine," he shouted excitedly.

Joe Dawson was the second to have his hand up, so he was asked to answer the question.

"My very best present was a train," said Joe shyly. His face turned a bright red. Annie felt sorry for wee Joe as she watched him quickly bury his head in his Mama's lap.

"What wonderful presents you have all received today! My best present was this tie," said the speaker, smiling as he lifted the tie for all to see.

"I found it in the toe of my stocking. How did Santa know the colour of my shirt?"

"Gifts make us very happy. We don't have to pay for them."

"God gave us a gift. It was His only Son, Jesus. That's the reason we are celebrating. It's His birthday today! Giving gifts reminds us that God gave the greatest gift of all.

"When you are given a gift, you take it and say, 'Thank you!'

"Have you taken God's gift? In order for it to be yours, you must take it!"

Something wonderful happened to Annie as everyone heartily sang the last carol, 'In the Bleak Mid-winter'. The last verse was to become very special to Annie...

"What can I give Him?
Poor as I am?
If I were a shepherd,
I would bring a lamb:
If I were a wise man,
I would do my part:
Yet what I can I give Him –
Give my heart"'.

Annie whispered to her Mama...

"Mama I have taken God's gift. As we sang the last verse of the carol, I gave Him my heart!"

Mrs. Pringle wanted to throw her arms around her daughter and tell her how delighted she was and that she had been praying for her, but she composed herself until after the benediction. Then, turning to Annie, she hugged her and said,

"Annie, I am so thrilled! My prayers have been answered. There is rejoicing in heaven! The Bible says, *There is joy in the presence of the angels of God over one sinner that repenteth!* Luke 15:10.

"Mama, that's where Papa is – 'in the presence of the angels', so he must be happy!"

Mother and daughter were smiling as they stepped out of the warm church into the blustering snow. Outside the church, Miss Diane was waiting for them for she wanted to congratulate Annie for reading the story of the birth of Jesus without making a mistake. Annie shared her news with Miss Diane, who threw her arms around her in a tight embrace and told she was thrilled that she had taken God's gift of Salvation.

Jenny Evans joined them and walked with Annie and her mother.

"I have a secret to share with you," she said shyly.

"Dave and I are engaged! There is no engagement ring, as you can see, for both of us decided we would put our small savings into our future together. You have been such wonderful friends that I wanted you to know. My family and a number of others already know. The news will soon spread around Millvale! Both our families are very happy about our engagement and planned marriage next year. No date is set yet, but we will tell you early in the new year!"

"Congratulations!" Mrs. Pringle and Annie spoke in unison as they excitedly congratulated Jenny and wished her God's blessing.

"My Mama is not very well this morning. I don't think it is anything serious – just a bad 'flu. I must hurry on to help Papa cook the Christmas dinner. I hope you will have a lovely time together today. It will not be easy for you, but we are praying that you will get strength to cope. God bless you!"

Jenny rushed on through the snow and the Pringles mingled among their friends. As they walked home, they received good cheer from many joyful people with smiles on their faces, while others came and hugged Mary and told her they would be praying for her.

Mary Pringle found it difficult to talk to those who had, like her family, suffered the loss of a father, a husband or a son, but she had found strength in being together with people who understood the meaning of grief and the devastation of war.

Passing the factory steps, Annie slipped a farthing into the almost empty tin box of an old, homeless man who lived on the doorstep of the factory.

When they arrived at their little house, Mrs Pringle brought the sack of presents into the parlour.

"'as Santa C'aus been?" asked Benny excitedly.

"Someone has been and left this sack," said Mama glancing at Annie's happy face.

"Look! I believe this parcel is for you."

Benny ripped off the wrapping paper and whooped in delight when the contents were revealed. "A bwight red fwire engine! Wook Mama! Shiny red fwire engine. BRUM, BRUM!"

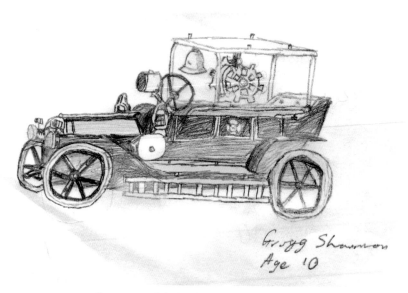

Gregg Shannon
Age 10

Benny was delighted with his fire engine!

Miss Hamley is Not Forgotten

The rest of the parcels were distributed and delight shone on the children's faces.

"A dolly and a skipping rope for me!" cried Heidi.

"And a lovely book and quill pen for me!" laughed Annie.

"What have you got Mama?"

"A beautiful creamy woollen shawl to keep me warm, my dear," smiled Mrs. Pringle.

"But look, there's one parcel left. Who could it be for?"

"Mama, why don't we give it to old Miss Hamley. She has no family and I'm sure she doesn't get any presents at all," suggested Annie.

"Why of course. What a nice idea, Annie," said Mrs. Pringle.

"We'll go over right away to her."

Several minutes later, they were outside Miss Hamley's cottage, which was just a few houses away from their home – it was the first house on Mill Row.

Mrs. Pringle tapped gingerly on the door. An old woman with silvery hair and a kind face stood in the doorway. Immediately, her face lit up with pleasure.

"How nice to see you! Happy Christmas!"

"Thank you! We just came to give you this Miss Hamley", began Mrs. Pringle, reddening slightly... I hope you don't think it's an awful cheek, but ..."

She held up the parcel and the old woman's face broke into a wide smile.

"Oh, how kind of you, my dears! Is it really for me?"

"Of course", replied Annie. "Take it, please."

After hesitating slightly, Miss Hamley accepted the parcel gratefully and opened it up.

"A bottle of cinnamon sweets! My favourites! Thank you so much. It was kind of you to think of me!"

Miss Hamley lived in the first house in Mill Row.

"Not at all," replied Mrs. Pringle, "glad it was a suitable present! Are you on your own this Christmas?"

"Yes, I am, but no matter, I don't really celebrate Christmas anymore."

"Don't you even have turkey and Christmas pudding?" asked Heidi, in wide-eyed innocence.

"No! I just boil an egg and butter a bit of bread. One of the scouts came and brought me down to the bakery, so I now have all I need for the moment," replied the old lady with a sigh. Then she brightened up again.

"I used to have family and we had happy times together. At least I have my memories!"

"Won't you come in for a while?"

"Err...we really should be getting back," said Mrs. Pringle, but as she saw the sadness in the lonely old lady's eyes, her heart went out to her.

"Perhaps you would like to come to our house for dinner. We really have too much to eat all by ourselves – thanks to an unexpected gift," and she winked at Annie.

"Oh, no! I couldn't intrude," frowned Miss Hamley. "I always say that Christmas is for families."

"You won't be intruding at all," Mrs Pringle assured her.

"We'd love to have you, really we would. Please come, Miss Hamley," pleaded Annie.

"Well... if you insist" - the elderly lady beamed! "I'll just fetch my coat. It's quite chilly outside."

Annie helped old Miss Hamley as they made their way back to the Pringle home for dinner. She again hoped she wasn't intruding into their private family Christmas, but Annie and her mother assured her they were really happy to have her company and would be delighted for her to be part of their Christmas celebrations. Heidi and Benny wanted to get back to play with their presents and also wanted to show old Miss Hamley what they got for Christmas.

A boy scout helped Miss Hamley carry her bread from the bakery

A Family of Five Again

Mrs. Pringle and Annie had made special decorations for the table. Christmas pictures had been cut from old Christmas cards and stuck unto the white serviettes. Annie had used her artistic skills to make place names for each of the family. They were colourful and added to the Christmas decorations on the table. She quickly prepared one for Miss Hamley while her mother was putting the finishing touches to the meal. The smell from the kitchen wafted into the room and made everyone feel hungry!

Soon the Pringle Christmas dinner was served and Mrs. Pringle thanked God for the good things and for their happy Christmas. There was turkey, gravy, stuffing, potatoes, vegetables, and the traditional Christmas pudding with custard for their desert.

As Miss Hamley slowly ate her portion and Heidi and Benny eagerly tucked into their meal, Mrs. Pringle whispered in Annie's ear...

"There are five of us for Christmas dinner!"

Annie understood, and nodded as they all tasted the steaming hot broth. It was so good after the cold outside.

There was quietness in the Pringle house! Heidi was the first to break the silence.

"Mama, this soup is so good! Do you like it Benny?"

"Yummy!" gulped Benny. He was so hungry, he had no time to talk!

The quietness gave Miss Hamley a chance to share some of her childhood memories.

Once her house had been neat and tidy with turf stacked in the shed, timber in neat piles beside it and the garden tools hanging in a row on the back wall of the shed. The snow was swept off the garden path on winter mornings, for Mr. Hamley was always afraid of someone slipping and getting hurt.

As Mrs. Pringle listened to old Miss Hamley, she remembered Father telling her that the Hamley home was the best kept home in Millvale.

"What you say is true, Miss Hamley," commented Mrs Pringle.

"Father told us to keep our house like the Hamley home, 'clean as a pin'!"

The villagers too used to say that the Hamley house was the cleanest in Millvale.

"Your father grew holly to decorate the house at Christmas. One Christmas my mother took me with her on her annual calls to friends. Your house was the most tastefully decorated house in Millvale, Miss Hamley, yet at no extra cost; there were flowers from the garden – your Papa planned his winter bloom with Christmas in mind! The door of 'Lee Cottage' had the most beautiful holly wreath tied with red wool. The 'Happy Christmas' sign was also plaited with strands of the red wool. Everyone commented on the artistic skills of the Hamley family!"

"My father was a quiet man," replied Miss Hamley thoughtfully. "You were a miracle baby! Your Mama nearly died at your birth. At that time, your Papa took over the cooking and some said your father continued to do the cooking, Miss Hamley."

Placing a huge bowl of roast potatoes on the table, Mrs. Pringle asked, "Is that right, Miss Hamley?"

"Because Mother's health was poor, Papa learned to cook. I was able to help him when I was older. We did it together. He always cooked the Christmas dinner."

At this stage, Mrs. Pringle had served the main course of the meal and everyone was enjoying the rich flavours of the turkey, the tender vegetables, the delicious onion stuffing and thick gravy.

"Oh Mama," said Annie, "This is the best turkey dinner I have ever tasted!"

"It's just like my father's." Miss Hamley's wrinkled face beamed as she tasted the rich gravy. Then she relived scenes of her childhood around the table in her cottage.

"I can picture Father, Mother my brother Jamie and Grandma Hamley around the table in our cottage," smiled Miss Hamley.

"There are five of us together again this Christmas. You are my family!"

Benny looked up from his turkey dinner and saw Miss Hamley laugh for the first time ever.

"Miss 'amley 'ike C'rimas, Mama!"

The Pringles agreed that Miss Hamley completed their family. She seemed a totally different person today and Mrs. Pringle was glad that Annie had remembered her.

Her stories held the children spellbound. She told how the snow was so deep one winter that her father could not see anything only snow when he opened the front door.

"How did you get out of your house?" asked Annie.

"Father went to the back door, where the snow was not just as deep. With the shovel and his bare hands, he made a small tunnel through the snow to the trees at the back of the house. It was mid-day before he was able to reach the shed to bring in the turf and logs. But he could not watch his family shiver in the cold. We just tried to keep going until we had a fire and were able to cook some food. I was your age Annie, and I was very frightened. I thought my little brother, Jamie, was going to die!

"He was so cold! Poor Betty kept telling me she was fainting. I really think it was that cold winter that led to Betty's death later for she was very ill and never fully recovered. The doctor said it was 'congestion of the lungs'. I remember Mother getting the warmest clothes in the house and piling them on us. Some of them were hand-downs from our late grandma, but they were warm. She wrapped each of us in blankets. But we were still cold. Mother became very ill a few days later and father thought she was going to die. For two weeks we nursed her. Her health improved in time for Christmas. That was a very special Christmas!

"Uncle Willie and Aunt Margaret invited our family to spend Christmas with them. Uncle Willie said the apple prices had been better than usual and our family would not have to bring any food or do any cooking. Their daughter Betty wanted her cousins to come for Christmas and had promised to work hard and help Mama to prepare a good Christmas dinner for the Hamley family.

"We had just washed the breakfast dishes when Uncle Willie arrived in his pony and trap. The neighbours watched as Father helped Mother into the trap and we proudly climbed in beside her. It was an hour's jaunt through the snow, but Uncle Willie had already made new tracks so it took less time for him to get us to the farm. Our cousins, Betty and Simon were as excited as we were. We brought some of our presents with us, and of course they let us play with their new toys. What fun we had! After dinner, we dressed in warm clothes and went out into the snow. Simon had a sleigh, so we became quite skilled after a few tumbles. We made the biggest snowman I have ever seen. We used stones for the eyes, and wood for the nose and mouth. We even made snow ears and pressed them on with our bare hands. Our hands felt like icicles! Aunt Margaret gave us some wool to use for hair: Simon got an old coat and a tie: he made a pipe and stuck it in his mouth. We felt we had broken the record for 'Snowman of the Year,' until Uncle Willie came to inspect him and announced that he and his brother had made a bigger one when they were boys!"

Heidi's eyes were glued on the old lady's face! She had an idea!

"Let's make a snowman after dinner, Annie!"

"That's a good idea, Heidi. Miss Hamley can be the judge and let us know if it's bigger than her snowman. Will you do that Miss Hamley?"

"Of course, dear, I would be so pleased to judge your snowman, and if it's bigger than the one we made at Springhill Farm, I will have to give you a prize."

There was great excitement about the snowman as Mama served up the Christmas pudding. Benny couldn't eat it, but the others asked for small portions, added a spoonful of cream and cleared the plates. It was so good! Annie helped Mama to clear the table and wash the dishes, while Miss Hamley watched Heidi and Benny play with their toys. Miss Hamley was so comfortable and content that she dozed off to sleep after half an hour.

At three o'clock in the afternoon, Mama got Benny dressed for the snow. He was only allowed out for a short time, but Heidi and Annie were told to come in when they felt cold. Mama opened the front door and three excited children left to build the greatest snowman in the world!

Annie had made a snowman with her father last Christmas, so she was able to show Heidi and Benny how to begin.

"We make the body first. O.K.?

"Let's roll a hard ball of snow with our hands. As it grows, we must shape it for the body."

Heidi decided she would start to make the snowman's head, but soon needed her big sister's help when a bulge started to form on the head - as it grew bigger, it became shapeless! Annie had to show Heidi again how to roll a round ball of snow.

Benny got so excited as the snowman's body grew! He started to roll it down the hill while Annie was helping Heidi. Suddenly, Annie turned to see Benny do a somersault over the ball of snow. A shriek went up as Benny was thrown into the deep snow and disappeared from view. His sisters rescued him, but a cold wet little boy had to be taken in to Mama. His tiny hands were almost numb with the cold, but a good wash in warm soapy water and a cuddle from Mama, soon brought a smile to his face again. He caught sight of his 'bwight red fwire engine' and forgot about making a snowman.

The Village becomes Alive

Annie and Heidi left Benny with Mama and Miss Hamley and returned to finish the showman. The Begley family saw them leave the house and came out to join them on the village hill. Soon the news spread around Millvale and before long, the small party had grown to a massive crowd. The boys of the village were glad of the opportunity for a bit of action. As the noise of merriment reached the families celebrating Christmas, enquiring faces appeared at the windows and soon doors opened and children and young people emerged to join in the fun. Because the houses were small and the community was closely knit, the scene changed from a quiet winter village scene to a truly boisterous Christmas party. Soon the whole village was united in the biggest event ever held in Millvale.

Even the Pepper boys, whose father owned the mill came to join in. They were home from boarding school and were glad of the opportunity to meet up with their former school friends. News reached the Pepper home of the now famous snowman. Mr. Pepper decided to offer a prize too. Brian and Evan Pepper brought the news to Annie. Their father had offered a five pound note if Miss Hamley decided   that the Millvale snowman was bigger than the one built at Springfield Farm! Excitement was building up as the villagers watched Annie and Heidi and their helpers try to lift 'Softy' upright to attach his head.

"All hands on deck," shouted Tom Begley. "Come everyone, we need help to lift Softy's body."

The older teenagers had returned with a pile of dry wood, so they threw it to the ground and rushed to help. Because they were not all lifting at the same time, they could not budge 'Softy's' body. Annie suggested that Tom Begley count to three and then shout 'lift'. It worked! His head was placed firmly on his big shoulders so they could add the finishing touches! The village bully, known as 'Tommy, the Terror', came forward with a hat, collar and tie for Softy. Jonnie Murphy brought a belt to tie round his waist and Bessie Begley brought three black buttons for his coat. Those who were not sleighing down the hill avoiding a collision with 'Softy' or away collecting firewood for a bonfire, were involved in some way helping the Pringle girls win the coveted prize.

In the late afternoon, while the children were playing on the village hill and Benny fully occupied with his 'bwight red fwire engine', Mrs. Pringle and Miss Hamley made themselves comfortable around the log fire for a friendly chat.

"Did you hear the news about Jenny Evans and Dave Armstrong, Miss Hamley?"

"No but I gather from the rumours around the village that there could be wedding bells in the not too distant future!"

"You're right! Jenny made her engagement public after church this morning. She is such a pretty girl! With her long dark hair and beautiful deep blue eyes she will make a beautiful bride. I will never forget her kindness to Annie, Miss Hamley," said Mrs. Pringle with a tear in her eye.

"When my dear Jack took Annie to the city by train to see the workhouse, he promised her he would take her back to see the big cathedral. But, sadly, he was called for military service and left before he had time to keep his promise. One day Jenny came to see me, after Jack was killed, and said that she would like to take Annie by train to the big city to fulfill her Papa's promise to his daughter. Annie had a wonderful day with Jenny. She is so knowledgeable, and told Annie a lot about the history of the cathedral. Annie told me it was built by Saint Patrick who brought Christianity to Ireland. He used the shamrock to teach the people about the trinity and people started to be educated after his preaching. It seems they wanted to learn to read and write. There were no pens like we have today, so Patrick taught them to write with a quill – a fowl's feather! They wrote on the skins of animals! Because of the great teaching of Patrick and others, Ireland became famous throughout the world and this small island of ours became known as 'The land of Saints and Scholars'."

"That's right Mrs. Pringle," said old Miss Hamley, who herself had been a school teacher.

"Scribes wrote the famous 'Book of Kells' and 'The Book of Armagh'. These are historic treasures which will be kept for every generation of people to learn from our history. Wealthy Americans are fascinated by 'The Book of Kells' and 'The Book of Armagh' when they come over here to try to trace their ancestry."

"I never heard the like of that Miss Hamley! I'm sure Jenny told Annie that too, but she told me so much about her visit to the city, that I think she forgot to finish her story. No doubt it will come out during the course of next year when she moves up to the higher class in school and learns more about history. Annie has her father's brain and wants to learn. I would love to be able to afford a good education for her, but that is not possible now that Papa is no longer with us."

Mrs. Pringle did not allow herself to become tearful, for little Benny was listening to the conversation and he was developing rapidly.

"Benny has a good brain. He too seems to have inherited his father's intelligence!"

"You are very modest, Mrs. Pringle," said Miss Hamley. You have so many excellent qualities and so many practical gifts! Don't undermine your abilities! Let's plan Jenny's wedding!"

"Annie and I would offer to help her to make the wedding dress, but Mrs. Evans is so talented that she will not need our help. As you know, Miss Hamley, Martha Evans is an expert with the needle, and, what's more, she doesn't even need a pattern! She just places the material on her kitchen table and cuts out each section of a garment – she never makes a mistake! Every garment is a perfect fit! What an amazing gift! It is a great saving for the family for Martha makes all the children's clothes, as well as sewing for others in Millvale."

Miss Hamley was enjoying the chat and waited for an opportunity to add her comment!

"Yes, and her mother and grandmother had the same talent. Obviously, it has been handed down from mother to daughter for generations. Jenny will continue the tradition of the most gifted dress-maker in the village!"

"Jenny has also her mother's baking skills. Her soda farls and wheaten bannocks are known to be the best in Millvale. Last week she came to see me and brought four soda farls and a wheaten bannock. They were so good - only lasted one day! The children told me they were better than mine!"

"You are an excellent baker too, Mrs. Pringle," interrupted Miss Hamley. "I enjoy your cooking and baking very much. Your talents are known in the village too! I think Mrs. Evans and Jenny would appreciate your help for the wedding. You can always bake for the wedding reception. Your sponge cakes are so light! There is nobody up to your standard in producing high quality apple pies, which are always very acceptable.

"A few dozen or two of them would be a welcome contribution."

Mrs. Pringle was deep in thought! She was remembering her own wedding to dear Jack.

"The late Mrs. Pepper, senior, made our wedding cake," she said with a tone of sadness. "Now both the Pepper parents and dear Jack are gone. How quickly our lives can be changed! But God has been good to us all and we must not complain, especially on Christmas Day!"

"I heard 'through the grape vine' that Mr. Pepper has allocated one of the larger houses on Chestnut Road to Dave's father? Because of his war injury, the stairs are much too difficult for him to climb. He called with the family and told them they could move into the larger house in the New Year. This will be a happier Christmas for the Andrews family!

"Mr. Pepper is like his father and grandfather – they were always considerate and good to their employees! He is going to rehabilitate victims of the war who were previously employed in the mill."

Mrs. Pringle's mind was busy!

"Perhaps Dave and Jenny will get the father's house! If my prediction is true, then we can all help the young couple decorate the house, for I know Martha Evans will do much of the wedding preparations herself. That would be wonderful, and I know other friends who would get involved. George Bingham is a good painter and decorator – he would gladly help them. Miss Hamley, I am getting excited for the young couple and their future in the Andrews home. I just hope I 'm right, but I must not get 'carried away'!"

Unexpected Visitors

Suddenly the work on the snowman stopped! All eyes were fixed on a pony and trap coming over the hill.

"Who is it?" shouted Danny Walsh.

Annie and Heidi got so excited. They recognized Uncle Ben and Aunt Sadie sitting sedately at the front of the trap. They knew that cousins Betty and Jonnie would be with them.

"Please carry on making 'Softy'. Heidi and I will be back in a few minutes. We must greet our cousins. They will join us to help put the finishing touches to the snowman!"

Annie and Heidi rushed off full of excitement to greet the unexpected visitors.

As the pony and trap came closer the children were waving frantically at each other. Uncle Ben had to control the horse but spared a second to give the two girls a wave.

Soon they came to a standstill outside the Pringle house and hugs and Christmas greeting were exchanged.

Uncle Ben and Aunt Sadie lived at Summerhill. They had a farm with a few cows and a big orchard. Much of their farm was bog land, so they had plenty of turf and supplied Jack and his family with turf every year. Ben Pringle was a lot older than his brother. In fact he was the oldest of a family of six boys, five of whom were killed at war. Ben had inherited the family farm and was like a father to his brothers. The others thought he spoiled Jack after the sudden and unexpected death of their father six years previously. He affectionately called him 'Wee Jack', even though he grew taller than his oldest brother!

Annie and Heidi visited the farm every year. They specially liked to go during the fruit season. Uncle Ben would not let them climb the trees, but he allowed them to gather the 'wind falls'. He always paid them, which meant Annie had to keep a note of the number of buckets of apples they gathered. The apple pickers at Summerhill Farm enjoyed having the children around. They sometimes brought them sweets and cookies! Visits to the farm were always fun times with their cousins.

Uncle Ben's Orchard

"I see you are all building a snowman," said Aunt Sadie, as she descended from the trap.

"We are having fun," replied Annie. Please Aunt Sadie, can Betty and Jonnie join us?"

"Of course they can, but let's first greet Auntie Mary and wish her a Happy Christmas."

Annie knocked the window!

"Mama, come! Open the door quickly! We have a big surprise," she shouted!

Mary Pringle's face lit up as she opened the door to the Ben Pringle family.

"Happy Christmas! Welcome Ben, Sadie, Betty and Jonnie!

"It is kind of you to come on Christmas Day!"

The Ben Pringle family returned their good wishes for Christmas. Previously, they had visited on St Stephen's day (Boxing Day), but obviously Ben was feeling the pain of Jack's death and wanted to see his youngest brother's family on Christmas Day, so decided to bring the two families together for the afternoon.

For Mary Pringle this was 'the icing on the cake'! Her dear Jack's family was always welcome, but more so in the circumstances. The girls and Jonnie disappeared through the door while the welcome visitors were taken to greet Miss Hamley.

The gifts were brought in and Uncle Ben took the horse to the back of the house where Jack had extended the wooden turf shed to provide shelter for the animal in winter.

Mary could only imagine the thoughts going through Ben's mind as she buttered the scones for refreshments for her welcome visitors. She went to the kitchen window and prayed for strength for both of them.

Ben stumbled as he released the tired horse from the trap. Jack always helped him with this; in fact, he always took over the job. It was Jack who took off the harness, dried the horse and gave him a well earned meal and drink.

Christmas brought memories of the past - Childhood fun: youthful pranks: hard work: romance and marriage: fatherhood, and brotherly companionship. The past year had brought changes, but life had to go on for the Pringles and the many other families robbed of a father or brother in the war. Ben braved himself and returned to the warmth of his brother's home.

In the excitement Benny was nearly forgotten. Not by Uncle Ben!

"Where's my boy?" were his first words as he came through the door.

He lifted the toddler in his strong arms and gave him a big Bear's hug. The child clung to him placing his arms tightly around his neck. Uncle Ben found it difficult to keep back the tears! He did release one hand to wipe his cheek, but quickly chatted to Benny, who took him to see his 'Bwight red fwire engine'.

Soon the four adults and wee Benny were enjoying the extra warmth of the coal from Uncle Ben's big sack, and Mary Pringle's hot mug of tea and fresh scones, with Aunt Sadie's home- made jam. The bright red raspberry jam blended with the seasonal red decorations!

Mary Pringle and Miss Hamley did not mind being interrupted in their wedding plans, so while Uncle Ben and Benny played with Benny's fire engine, the women exchanged news items with gusto.

High on their agenda were the preparations for Christmas and the two mothers' total exhaustion: then it was the size of the turkey, the success of the Christmas cake and most important, the steamed pudding. The women of Millvale talked more about their steamed pudding than they did about their Christmas cake! Miss Hamley was the last to speak on the subject, by declaring that Mary Pringle's pudding was the best in Millvale!

The weather had been favourable for the farming community in the county, and the Bramley apple prices had never been better: the good weather had enabled the Ben Pringle family to cut and bring in more turf than on any previous year. Both families benefited from this and were thankful to God for His provision.

"God kept His promise," commented Miss Hamley. "The Bible tells us that 'seedtime and harvest will not fail'. He provides for the sparrows and he provides for us!"

Sadie Pringle and Miss Hamley had been in the teaching profession, so education was the next topic of conversation. They both lamented that recent changes in the education system were a disaster!

As Sadie Pringle listened to the wisdom of the elderly woman, her mind sprung into action...

"You are absolutely right, Miss Hamley - the government has spent too much money on the war and not bothered to focus on educating the future generation." Neither of them had a solution to the problem, but at least it helped to air their views. Mary named some of Miss Hamley's past pupils who had become famous, which gave the three of them a sense of pride in the local achievements. They discussed the Bronte sisters and Joseph Scriven, whose names were of local interest, being from their neighbouring county. The two concerned mothers agreed they would have to wait to see if the changes would produce better results. Uncle Ben looked up and nodded his head in agreement. He was occupied with Benny in pretending to be a fireman. They had a big fire to attend to and that was more important to a toddler than education!

Aunt Sadie opened her handbag and brought out a photo.

"Our neighbour, John Bradley, took this photo of Jack and a few friends, who went for a ride around his farm on the way back from church one Sunday. It was just a few weeks before Jack left for the war," said Aunt Sadie, handing Mary a photo. "I thought you would like to keep it, so I brought it to you for Christmas!"

Mary took the photo in her hands with a smile on her face.

"Sure enough," she said, as she handed the photo to Miss Hamley. "There's my Jack sitting on the right with his legs dangling over the side of the trap. Oh, Sadie, I will treasure that! We could not even afford a photo of our wedding. The children will be so pleased to have a picture of their Papa. It must have been taken during the apple picking season last year. That's you Sadie, sitting behind Papa. I can remember it was a lovely sunny autumn day, so I told Papa I would take the baby, and the girls home to Uncle Ben's farm and get the dinner ready for us all. You objected, Sadie, for you wanted me to go with Jack, but you needed a break and I won the argument! John Bradley said he would have you back in half an hour, but, if my memory serves me, it was over an hour! Dear Jack so enjoyed the chat and the visit to the Bradley farm. He talked about it often before he left for the Front."

Benny was on his feet – he wanted to see the photograph.

"Papa! U'kle Ben, 'ook!" Uncle Ben was so moved he could not speak, but fortunately Benny did not notice.

"'Ook, Mama, 'ers Papa." He pointed to Papa's peak cap with his tiny finger. There was a marked silence in the room! Quickly Uncle Ben took the photo and told Benny all about John Bradley's farm and promised that when he would visit next year, he would ask John to take Benny for a drive too.

Excitement Mounts in Millvale

While most of the children were building the snowman, some of the older teenagers disappeared into the woods outside the village and brought back wood. It was wet with the snow, but they had gone to their homes and begged for turf and dry wood to build a bonfire.

Danny Taylor and Jonnie Burnside had headed up the search and everyone was surprised at the amount of wood and rubbish they had piled up for the 'big event' of judging 'Softy'!

Soon the fire was ready and the scene was set to judge the snowman. All ages had gathered - even babies snuggly wrapped in warm blankets and toddlers in winter clothes and boots, were beside their parents. Everyone revived after their big Christmas dinner to enjoy the celebration and await the arrival of Miss Hamley.

With Softy standing tall on the village hill, Mrs. Pringle brought old Miss Hamley to judge the big fellow! She could hardly believe what she saw! Her mouth fell open and she was lost for words!

Eventually, she got her breath back, and said.

"Children. I have never seen such a big snowman! He should be called, 'Softy the giant Snowman'."

Clarke Neville
age 10

Miss Hamley suggested that they call him...
" 'Softy' The GIANT Snowman!"

The villagers all gathered around 'Softy', and with the snow still falling they danced around him, singing with gusto.

For he's a jolly good fellow!
For he's a jolly good fellow!
For he's a jolly good fellow!
And so say all of us!

Even Benny joined in... 'olly good fello'!

Heidi tugged at Mama's coat, as she called to Annie.

"There's Mr. Pepper!"

Nobody saw him come down the hill, because the snow was falling even thicker and faster. Besides, all eyes were on 'Softy'.

A cheer went up from the crowd as the respected gentleman pulled up beside the Pringle family and Miss Hamley. Then in unison, the villagers, including Benny, began to clap their hands. He was enjoying the fun, but didn't really understand what was happening.

" 'P'eas 'ift Benny, Mama! 'Benny see Peppi'!"

Mrs. Pringle asked Ben and Sadie to look after Miss Hamley and lifted Benny in her arms. Mr. Pepper had a large white envelope in his hand. He made a short speech and thanked the Pringle family for bringing such happiness to the village at Christmas. Then he handed Annie the envelope and wished everybody a Happy Christmas. Annie opened the envelope and read the big Christmas card...

"The Pepper family wishes to thank Annie Pringle and the family for bringing joy to the village in what has been a difficult year for us all. We have lost many of our sons and fathers at war, but today you have proved that there is strength to cope in tragic circumstances. You have brought together a village that was in mourning this Christmas and our families have enjoyed a fun day. My family join me in wishing you all a Happy Christmas and a Peaceful New Year!"
Signed: William Alexander Pepper.

There was silence as Annie finished reading the card and held up the five pound note for all to see. Then, bracing herself, she found strength: although still shocked, she spoke with clear diction. She thanked Mr. Pepper and wished him and his family a happy and peaceful Christmas and new year. Annie could feel her hand shaking as she held the money!

It was Mr. Pepper whose strong voice relieved a now tense atmosphere...

"Three cheers for this remarkable family! Hip! Hip! Hooray!" Everybody was stunned, but after a solo cheer from Mr. Pepper, the villagers joined in...

"Hip! Hip! Hooray! Hip! Hip! Hooray!"

The crowd started to clap again as Mr. Pepper climbed into his pony and trap and left his family with the villagers to chat before breaking up the celebration. He waved as they watched him disappear up the hill and vanish from view.

Mr. Pepper, the mill owner, lived on a large estate at the top of the village hill and could often be seen riding in his pony and trap.

Miss Hamley was delighted about the big prize. She knew this would mean so much to the Pringle family. It would be an unexpected bonus to start the New Year. Mrs. Pringle could not believe it!

Bessie Begley was beside Annie when she received the envelope. She was so pleased for her friend and wanted her to know how pleased she was that she had received the prize...

"Congratulations! You deserve that for you have a heart of gold!" She smiled as she continued...

"Look Annie, the two Pepper girls are here with their older brothers. Rachel and Judith are so pretty!"

Annie had not been aware of them. Suddenly, she spotted Mrs. Dorothy Pepper and her sister Eva - beside her was her husband, David, and their three daughters, Rachel, Judith and Mary. They had honoured the villagers with their presence on what to them was a very special family gathering. Everyone had spotted them except Annie who was overwhelmed with the crowd gathered around the bonfire!

"If only Papa had been here to witness this, Bessie! It would have made me the happiest girl in the world. Do you think he can see it from heaven?"

"I don't know, but I do hope he knows you are coping and having fun!"

"Please call to see Bruno before you go into your house!"

Annie was overjoyed! Now she knew that the new Begley puppy was called Bruno.

"Oh, Bessie," said Annie, "I was so happy for you! This morning I heard him bark and knew your happiness would be restored. I will ask

Mama if I can go in to play with him for a little while. Do you mind if Heidi and Benny come too? They want to meet Bruno."

"Of course you can bring Heidi and Benny and if Miss Hamley and your Mama want to meet Bruno, we can bring him into your house. But he is very frisky and might jump up on Miss Hamley's knee!"

"Let's see what Mama says", said Annie. "It might be too much excitement for one day for old Miss Hamley!"

"You're right Annie! We can visit Miss Hamley tomorrow and take Bruno to see her. He is so tiny and such a cuddly little puppy. He knows his name already, Annie. I just love him! Santa could not have brought me a better gift. Come quickly and meet him!"

Bruno Meets the Family

Mama had given consent for Bruno to be introduced to the Pringle family, and Miss Hamley. There was great excitement as the tiny little black puppy bounded through the door and licked everyone excitedly before jumping onto Miss Hamley's lap! Mrs. Pringle had to rescue him! Everyone knew there were happy days ahead in the New Year with Bruno living next door!

Mrs. Pringle insisted that Miss Hamley only give her children one sweet each as the cinnamon sweets were her special Christmas surprise treat. Miss Hamley reluctantly agreed, but insisted that she give one to Betty and Jonnie too. Everyone agreed!

In her own unique manner, Miss Hamley proudly presented Annie, Heidi and Benny with their reward. As she gave one to Betty and Jonnie she sheepishly looked at Mrs. Pringle and with a twinkle in her eye, passed the cinnamon sweets to the Begley children. Bruno gave a sharp bark and bounded forward – he too wanted a cinnamon sweet!

Bruno meets his new neighbours at No. 7

Annie opened the envelope which contained the brand new five pound bank note!

"Mama you have given us all a wonderful Christmas," said Annie, as she gave her the five pound note. Thank you for being a wonderful Mama!"

Miss Hamley made a little speech expressing her appreciation for the Pringle family's kindness and congratulating the children on 'The Biggest Snowman in the World'! Benny was the first to clap his hands. Soon the house was full of merriment and celebration. Everyone had had a HAPPY CHRISTMAS! There were hugs all round and a hot cup of cocoa warmed everyone up.

Uncle Ben offered to accompany Miss Hamley to her home, while the family packed up to leave for the farm. Annie offered to go with him to carry the hurricane lamp in front of Miss Hamley lest she would trip and fall. Bessie Begley lifted Bruno and suggested that all the children go and accompany Miss Hamley to her home. It was a happy Miss Hamley, who took Uncle Ben's arm, and escorted by a high-spirited group of children, she was on her way.

The two Mrs. Pringles were alone in the house with a tired little toddler curled up on the sofa – Benny was fast asleep! It had been a full day for him but he kept going until the last half hour. Miss Hamley had proved she was still young in spirit by entering into the Christmas festivities with the enthusiasm of a teenager! She would not easily forget her Christmas with the Pringle family.

"I don't know how you managed to get everyone into the house Mary?" said Aunt Sadie.

"The house is small but the welcome is great," replied Mary Pringle with a smile. "It was too bad Ben and the boys had to be in the kitchen, but with Bruno bounding from one to the other, it was impossible for everyone to fit into the parlour!"

Frost and Snow

I love the frost of the winter,
it reminds me of childhood and home:
a warm glowing fire and the family
chatting freely, when day's work is done!
I see Mama relaxed in the corner,
Dad with his feet on the hob!
Little Jimmy, with teddy and puppy,
content to be left on his own!
I recall the utter contentment
knowing Jack Frost was outside
knocking on doors and on windows,
preparing the ground for our slide!

I love the snow of the winter,
bringing freshness and vigour to life:
It purifies – spreads a clean blanket
on the deadness that autumn has left:
It speaks of the cross of the Saviour –
precious blood that was shed for me
to bring pardon and peace to my conscience,
refreshing and setting me free!
Though your sins be as red as crimson,
they can be cleansed white as snow –
this is the wonderful message
God wants every sinner to know!

Frost and Snow

Mary Pringle was happy to have her dear Jack's family to enjoy the fun. Sadie had such understanding of her sister-in-law's pain and loss. As a wife and mother, she felt the pain herself and was happy that Ben decided to make the journey on Christmas Day.

"Jack has had his first Christmas in Heaven," said Sadie after a short silence. She felt lost for words for she knew Mary had come back to the reality of the vacant chair. Mary's eyes were fixed on the chair Miss Hamley had vacated - that was her dear Jack's chair. Sadie's voice interrupted her thoughts. There was a tear in her eye as she turned to reply to Sadie's comments.

"Yes, I know he is happy, but there is sorrow in my heart. This would have been our fifteenth Christmas together, Sadie. Every Christmas was different, and every Christmas was special. He would have enjoyed Benny more this year, for he is now expressing his thoughts so clearly. Jack would have loved to hear him say, 'bwight red fwire engine'. Your visit has meant that Uncle Ben has enjoyed hearing him use new words and expand his childish vocabulary. God has been good to us all and provided for us in a remarkable way. I am happy that the children had lots of presents and a very happy Christmas."

Voices outside announced the return of Ben and the children. The three Begley children and Bruno came in to say their 'Goodbyes'. Bruno leaped onto Aunt Sadie's lap and gave her a lick on the cheek. It frightened her but soon the little puppy nestled down and obviously felt comfortable on her knee. The children thought he was so cute. They were down on the floor watching to see how long he would stay and what he would do next. Bruno did not give them the response they expected and began to yawn. He too had had a long day so decided it was time for a nap!

It was Bessie who moved first for she could see Uncle Ben was looking at the clock.

"I think it's time to take Bruno home. What an exciting day this has been! Thank you all for the fun we have enjoyed together. This has been a very happy Christmas, because you have all made it special!"

Tom picked Bruno up and soon the three Begley children were gone. The Pringle family started to pack up while Mama made a fresh pot of tea and brought in the Christmas cake. There had been so much food earlier that nobody wanted cake - now it was different as eager eyes caught sight of the decorative traditional cake. Annie had cut out small pictures from a magazine and stuck them on the top. There was a Christmas tree, a balloon, two Santas. Mama had written Happy Christmas with red icing. When Bruno had bounded into the room he had wakened Benny, who seemed to get a new lease of life.

"Benny want C'rim'as cake, Mama! Peas, me want 'is pice with Santa!"

Everyone laughed as Mama served Uncle Ben and Benny first!

"I see you treat the men with respect, too!" observed Aunt Sadie. "Grandma Pringle spoiled her boys for their future wives. But we must not grumble for they work very hard and deserve to be treated well!" Nobody objected as they savoured Mama's Christmas cake. There were expressions of – "Yummy! Delicious!" These were the comments needed to assure Mary Pringle of the total satisfaction of the whole Pringle family.

"You two women must have talked while we were out doing our good turn for the day! No packing done, Sadie? Typical! I suppose I have to make allowances because of the number of times you get the opportunity to talk during the year. We really must leave my dear so please have everything ready when I hitch up the cart and feed the horse. It's getting late for the children. Besides I have a few farm jobs to do before bedtime and everyone is exhausted. There's going to be a big frost tonight!"

Uncle Ben disappeared to feed his horse, light the carbide cart lights, and prepare for home. Meanwhile Aunt Sadie fetched the coats, scarves and gloves, to be ready to leave as soon as Ben came back. It was difficult to say 'Goodbye', but it was a happy ending to a day of surprises.

Carbide trap lights were used to illuminate the trap or cart.

What Christmas is all About

Both Heidi and Benny were exhausted and within minutes were fast asleep. Mrs. Pringle and Annie washed the few remaining cups in the basin and sat down at the fire. As they watched the last flickers from a burning log, they seemed to know each others thoughts. Mrs. Pringle closed her eyes and Annie knew that meant she wanted time to be alone with her thoughts. Annie picked up a piece of paper to write down some of her thoughts on the first Christmas without Papa - she stopped writing and looked up.

"Mama, do you think it really was Santa Claus who sent all those lovely gifts today!"

"We may never know, my dear, who left the presents, but I've learnt what Christmas is all about."

Annie stopped writing and looked up,

"What's that Mama?"

Mrs. Pringle turned to look at her daughter again - young and full of innocence. As Annie's wide eyes looked up at her Mama questioningly, Mrs. Pringle hugged her daughter and said,"One thing you always need to remember in life is that no matter what your situation is, there is always somebody worse off than yourself. It's your job to help them. Up until this morning the only people I was thinking of were my family and myself. I forgot about all the Miss Hamleys of this world!"

"What is the real meaning of Christmas then, Mama?"

Mrs. Pringle smiled and said ... "'The Spirit of Giving'!"

Luke: 2, 1 – 20
Alternative Translation

Christ born of Mary

And it came to pass in those days, that a decree went out from Caesar Augustus, that all the world should be registered.
This census first took place when Quirinius was governing Syria.
So all went to be registered everyone to his own city.
Joseph also went up from Galilee, out of the city of Nazareth, into Judea, to the city of David, which is called Bethlehem, because he was of the house and lineage of David
to be registered with Mary his betrothed wife, who was with child.
So it was, that while they were there, the days were completed that she should be delivered.
And she brought forth her first born son, and wrapped him in swaddling clothes, and laid him in a manger, because there was no room for them in the inn.

Glory in the Highest

Now there were in the same country shepherds living out in the fields, keeping watch over their flocks by night.
And behold, an angel of the Lord stood before them, and the glory of the Lord shone around them, and they were greatly afraid.
Then the angel said unto them,
"Do not be afraid, for behold, I bring you good tidings of great joy which shall be to all people.
"For there is born this day to you this day in the city of David a Saviour, who is Christ the Lord.
"And this will be a sign to you: You will find the babe wrapped in swaddling clothes, lying in a manger.
And suddenly there was with the angel a multitude of the heavenly host praising God and saying,

"Glory to God in the highest,
And on earth peace,
goodwill toward men!"
So it was, when the angels had gone away form them into heaven, that the shepherds said one to another, "Let us now
go to Bethlehem and see this thing that has come to pass, which the Lord has made known unto us".

And they came with haste, and found Mary, and Joseph, and the babe lying in a manger.

And when they had seen Him, they made widely known the saying which was told them concerning this child.

And all they that heard it marvelled at those things which were told them by the shepherds.

But Mary kept all these things and pondered them in her heart.

Then the shepherds returned, glorifying and praising God for all the things that they had heard and seen, as it was told them.